"I've never felt anything like this before,"

Jack murmured.

If he'd dumped a bucket of live bait on Anita, it couldn't have broken the spell any quicker. She jerked her hands from beneath his shirt and pushed him away. "You can come up with a better one than that, Jack Hayden. Anyone who kisses like you do has felt like this before. Plenty of times!"

"But I haven't," he protested.

"You've certainly had enough opportunities, though, haven't you?"

"How many opportunities have you had, Anita?"

She took a deep breath and answered just as quietly, "Enough."

"Enough to know what you want?"

"I don't want anything, remember? You can kiss like the dickens, Jack Hayden, but I'm not interested."

Dear Reader,

Welcome to the fourth great month of CELEBRATION 1000! We're winding up this special event with fireworks!—six more dazzling love stories that will light up your summer nights. The festivities begin with *Impromptu Bride* by beloved author Annette Broadrick. While running for their lives, Graham Douglas and Katie Kincaid had to marry. But will their hasty wedding lead to everlasting love?

Favorite author Elizabeth August will keep you enthralled with *The Forgotten Husband.* Amnesia keeps Eloise from knowing the real reason she'd married rugged, brooding Jonah Tavish. But brief memories of sweet passion keep her searching for the truth.

This month our FABULOUS FATHER is *Daniel's Daddy*—a heartwarming story by Stella Bagwell.

Debut author Kate Thomas brings us a tale of courtship—Texas-style in—*The Texas Touch.*

There's love and laughter when a runaway heiress plays *Stand-in Mom* in Susan Meier's romantic romp. And don't miss Jodi O'Donnell's emotional story of a love all but forgotten in *A Man To Remember.*

We'd love to know if you have enjoyed CELEBRATION 1000! Please write to us at the address shown below.

Happy reading!

Anne Canadeo
Senior Editor

Please address questions and book requests to:
Silhouette Reader Service
U.S.: 3010 Walden Ave., P.O. Box 1325, Buffalo, NY 14269
Canadian: P.O. Box 609, Fort Erie, Ont. L2A 5X3

THE TEXAS TOUCH

Kate Thomas

Published by Silhouette Books
America's Publisher of Contemporary Romance

To my husband, Tom, and to Joice Smith,
the two people who loved me best.
Thanks is too small a word.

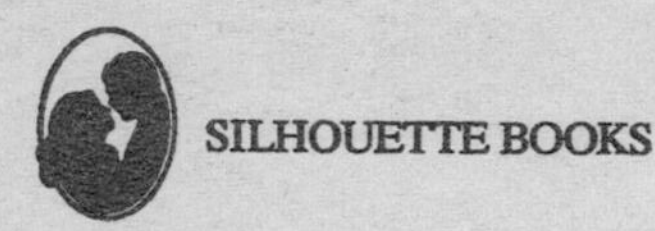

ISBN 0-373-19023-9

THE TEXAS TOUCH

This edition published by arrangement with Harlequin Enterprises B.V.

Printed in U.S.A.

KATE THOMAS

As a Navy brat, I moved frequently until I was lucky enough to attend college in Texas. I married a native Texan, produced another and remain fascinated by language and cultural diversity. With my writing, I like to celebrate one trait all humans share: a desire to love and be loved.

Dear Reader,

The Texas Touch is my first book for Silhouette Romance and it's a dream come true. I've loved reading since before I could read; writing seems the most enviable occupation, being published the most exciting achievement imaginable.

I came to Texas to attend college. The week after I arrived, the schools were closed due to *rain.* (Well, it was actually the outskirts of a hurricane.) The first Texan phrase I learned was, "Honey, we sure don't." It was the most positive negative I'd ever heard!

Over the years, I've come to appreciate the Lone Star state's unique charm. Where else will you find a motorcycle-riding grandmother as governor? Or a school whose graduates would be so proud of winning an Olympic gold medal, they'd have it bronzed? (Just kidding, Aggies.)

I can't thank Silhouette enough for this opportunity. I hope *The Texas Touch* conveys to my readers some small sense of our warm, friendly people, our customs and beliefs.

Living in Texas and getting paid to write about ordinary, wonderful people experiencing the eternal, ever-new joy of falling in love—honey, it sure doesn't get any better than this!

Gratefully yours,

Kate Thomas

Chapter One

Jack donned sunglasses against the bright July morning and turned the rental car's radio to a country music station. He exited the San Antonio airport and traveled rapidly past a typical downtown of skyscrapers, past miles of suburban tract homes, then fields of sunburned crops and pastures dotted with cows clumped under stumpy, twisted trees.

His goal was straight ahead, just south of the Alamo City. Like thousands before him, Jack "Hollywood" Hayden was coming to Texas looking for a new start in life—as a teacher and football coach.

At least, that was the plan. After four years, it was good to have one again. Granting his request for a Saturday interview was a favorable omen, too, he told himself.

Sailing down the highway, Jack cringed at the thought of the arrogant young fool he'd once been. While millions of people watched on television, he'd actually said *"I'd rather wrestle a cobra in a barrel of roaches than get married."* Even flushed with a Super Bowl victory in his rookie year of professional football and too young to know better, it was unforgivable. After a blindside tackle had crushed his knee on the first play of his second season, he'd never had a chance to redeem his reputation.

As for forgetting— The media in several large urban areas had mentioned it prominently during periodic whatever-happened-to features that rehashed his flamboyant past in discouraging detail. He'd lost a dull but possible relationship that way.

Jack focused on the present. If this interview went well, he might be lucky enough to lapse into anonymity at last and pursue an ordinary life, maybe find a wife, get married, have children. It wasn't such a big dream; he'd finally realized he didn't need a big city to make it come true. A nice medium-size town would have a good pool of prospects. Hopefully, in the town up ahead—Larson, Texas—he'd receive a year's contract to teach and coach. Then he'd have twelve months to meet lots of unmarried, unattached women who'd never heard of his glamour-boy reputation or that stupid quote.

Jack knew just where to meet those women, too. He'd join a health club, ask for advice in the produce section of the grocery store—he'd sign up for the library guild if he had to!

Reality had taught Jack some painful, but valuable lessons. He didn't expect the moon anymore. As long as one of the prospects was compatible in most ways and she'd have him, that was enough for Jack. Love was for the lucky and the deserving; he'd disqualified himself with his big ego and his reckless behavior. Now, he'd settle for companionship and a chance to have a family.

He wasn't asking too much, was he?

Despite the long vistas of empty countryside drooping in the July heat, Jack's spirits continued to rise as he left the past behind and headed toward his future.

An hour beyond San Antonio, he turned off the wide, smooth four-lane highway at the sign pointing to his destination: Larson, Texas. *Here we go,* he thought, a butterfly of anticipation fluttering in his stomach.

The road dipped under a railroad trestle, then curved and rose. One by one, the first buildings appeared: an old house trailer, a small frame house, an abandoned building with an Ice House sign above its sagging, torn screen door....

Jack's heart sank, his disappointment grew as he drove slowly down the main street. Four blocks. The whole town was four blocks long. Larson had a bank, a post office, a laundromat, a feed store and a meat market. Not even a grocery store.

As if it had a mind of its own, the rental sedan pulled in beside a beat-up pickup truck in front of the meat market. It seemed to be the only place inhabited, judging by the otherwise empty street. Jack switched off his engine and listened to the silence. Even when he closed his eyes and leaned his forehead against the steering wheel, Jack could see clearly—he'd made another mistake.

"No, the same one, chump," he muttered as he unbuckled his seat belt. "Twenty-seven years old and you haven't learned yet! You didn't do any research on this place, did you? You just opened your mouth without connecting it to your brain. It's the second of July already—too late to find another coaching position. You're going to have to take this one, if they offer it to you. You're going to be stuck for a year in Nobody's Home, Texas. So much for your meeting-women plan." Jack sighed and unfolded himself from the car.

He stepped up on the sidewalk carefully—his knee was unreliable after long periods of inaction. After another disheartening look up and down the deserted street, he entered the market's quiet gloom.

"Can I help you?" the man behind the counter asked, except it came out sounding more like "Kin ah hep ya?"

Jack managed to translate the Texas accent and answered, "I'm looking for the high school."

The man nodded. "Vern Smolik," he said and stretched his hand across the top of the glass-fronted meat case. "Pleased to meet'cha. You Jack Hayden?" he asked.

"Yes." Jack braced himself. Would the man make some critical reference to Jack's past?

"I'm also president of the school board and we're scheduled to interview each other in about an hour," Smolik said. "But right now, I'm on the meat committee for the Larson Volunteer Fire Department Fourth of July fund-raising picnic, so—" He gestured at the butcher block behind him. It was piled with succulent slabs of ribs, coiled ropes of sausages and long, thick cuts of beef—all beautifully cooked and emitting the most tantalizing odor.

"I apologize, son," the man continued. "Doris wasn't looking at the calendar when she scheduled your interview, but if you don't mind the informality, this'll be a good chance for you to meet and get to know us."

"Sounds fine to me," Jack said with a sigh of relief. So far, so good. No references to his past. Casual was more his style, anyway—if he could remember to think before he spoke.

"Well, come on back and help me load up this meat, then we'll get it over to the picnic, so they can start feeding the hungry hordes."

Yeah, all five of them, Jack thought as he obligingly came behind the counter, folding back the sleeves of his pale blue dress shirt and loosening his tie.

As Jack followed Smolik through town a few minutes later, he made himself shrug off his initial disappointment. If he'd learned anything during the last four years, it was that instant gratification wasn't a birthright.

They turned on to a highway that intersected Larson's main street and there was the high school. The butcher slowed down as they drove past. As he'd promised, Jack could pretty much see everything from the road.

The Larson Combined Middle and High School consisted of four buildings forming a square, backed by a large, new-looking metal gymnasium and athletics fields. Surrounding the school were fields of corn and soybeans. Across the highway was a Dairy Queen, a gas station advertising diesel fuel and a deer processing plant. The view confirmed Jack's first impression of the town: Larson was too small. There probably wasn't an eligible woman within miles.

Jack accelerated to catch Smolik's truck as it turned left down a narrow paved road. Well, he didn't want to go back to selling sporting goods or teaching shop to three bored kids at Wyler Military Academy. He wanted to get back into the field he loved, so he'd do his best to land this job.

A year of experience at Larson High would look better on his résumé than none. Somehow, one year of playing professional football didn't seem to count for much when it came to landing secondary-school coaching positions.

What did he expect? After that one incredible year when he'd come off the bench and led his team to the Super Bowl, Jack's luck hadn't been so hot. Maybe he'd used it all up.

He shrugged off a wave of despair. He hadn't seen another car since leaving the highway—except Smolik's truck. Was all the meat they'd loaded going to be wasted at this picnic, which the school-board president said was a fund-raising event? Probably hoping to raise enough money to buy a garden hose!

"Jesse, would you please watch the little ones for Aunt Isabel?" Anita's exasperation was only indirectly related to her brother's halfhearted execution of his baby-sitting duties. She could blame the heat, but Anita knew the real source of her outburst. A few sharp words felt better—momentarily, anyway—than tears. She just couldn't find a way to reach Jesse, to help him find a way out of his continuing grief.

Face it, Anita: a moping, withdrawn seventeen-year-old isn't the world's best baby-sitter, but you're not exactly the world's greatest instant parent, either. Jesse won't talk to you. Won't respond to anything. It's as though he died, too. How do you bring him back to life? You'd better think of something soon.

"Aw, 'Nita. They're okay. They're playing with their friends, for gosh sakes! What does she expect from me?" the boy grumbled as he walked off, but Anita knew he was headed back to duty. Jesse was a good kid, really, but between adolescent hormones and the shock of the house fire that had killed their parents in January, he was a handful.

One of these days, Anita needed to do some grieving of her own.

But not today. Today, she'd keep busy serving barbecue plates and remember fondly all the years her mother had been behind this table, dishing up mounds of potato salad, pinto beans and Smolik's barbecue brisket. Even during her years in San Antonio, Anita had never missed the annual Larson celebrations, despite her city friends' incredulity at her simple tastes.

"I asked for sausage, Anita," a voice insisted as its owner pushed the plate back at her.

"Sorry, Glen," Anita said, wielding her tongs to exchange ribs for sausage. "Sauce?"

"No, thanks. You staying for the dance later?" Glen Baker looked at her hopefully. He was ten years older than Anita, divorced, overweight and balding. Nobody to set a woman's heart aflutter.

Well, there wasn't *anyone* in Larson that set her heart aflutter, Anita thought wryly. And heartthrob material wouldn't be interested in a twenty-five-year-old school nurse with custody of a morose brother in the throes of adolescence and facing four years of college tuition.

Romance was simply not in the cards for her. Anita sighed, nodded to Glen and turned her attention to the next person in line.

Jack stared through the windshield in disbelief. He'd followed Vern Smolik through the deserted edges of town, thinking dire thoughts about the headhunter who'd directed his application to this tiny town. Now, he found himself stuck in a traffic jam any urban area would be proud of. There was a line of at least twenty vehicles, mostly trucks, in front of him, and more behind.

After they all crawled onto a grassy field and parked, he eased his knee into a weight-bearing position, then hurried over to Vern's truck to help unload the huge pans of cooked meat. It looked as if the volunteer firemen were going to need every sliver.

"Let's get this delivered, then we can grab a plate lunch for ourselves and have a little talk."

"Fine, Mr. Smolik." He'd done plenty of interviews but never at a sweltering Texas picnic. The crowd was, of course, mostly couples and families with small children, but they looked friendly. *Normal.* Maybe a year in such a small place wouldn't be so bad, after all. Another year for people to forget what an idiot he'd been, a year to get some real coaching experience.... "This is quite a turnout. Did you expect such a crowd?"

"We sell out every year," Vern proclaimed proudly. "Larson's the best little town in Texas. We do a heck of a job supporting our civic organizations, Jack."

"So I see." They worked their way through the stream of people headed toward a huge striped tent at the center of the picnic site, identified by a tall wooden sign as the County Fairgrounds.

"Where do you want it, Elly?" Vern asked when they reached the tent. Elly was a large woman wearing a denim skirt and a T-shirt that read Firefighters Are Hot Stuff.

"Vern! Thank heavens! We're just about out of brisket already. Who's your helper?"

"Oh, Elly, this is Hollywood Hayden," Vern said as he thumped his burden down on a table. "Elly Janek—she's in charge of the food."

His life as Hollywood Hayden was over. "Jack," he said firmly, shaking Elly's hand politely. It was plain old Jack from now on. "Jack Hayden. Pleased to meet you."

"Okay, Jack it is," Vern said, accepting the hint, then asked the dinner chairwoman again, "Where do you want the meat?"

With Elly directing, Jack and Vern worked their way to the far end of the row of tables lining one side of the tent.

"Here comes the cavalry," Vern announced, then addressed the woman nearest the depleted serving platters. "Put the rest of those links in here, Anita, and make room for my assistant. He's got the brisket."

Between the crowd, the heat and the long drive from San Antonio, Jack was concentrating solely on maintaining his balance and not dropping the meat. When he saw the small hands efficiently clearing a space on the table, he was only thinking about safely depositing the huge metal pan piled high with mouth-watering barbecue.

Once it was firmly set in place, he had time to look at the person who belonged to the hands.

Not a person, a vision! A vision of female perfection. Small, but not too small. Young, but not too young. Hair like polished ebony in a smooth, straight style that swung just above her shoulders with every movement of her head, luminous dark eyes, a mouth made for kissing, curves in all the right places.

"Hi, I'm Jack Hayden. And you're—?" *Please don't be married,* he begged silently as he waited for her reply.

"Anita Valdez," the vision said without looking at him. She was busy filling plates with the meat they'd delivered, her tongs flashing.

"Can you make us up a couple of plates, Anita?" Vern interjected. Jack was silent, stunned. "We can cut in line, since we're kind of privileged characters, aren't we, Jack?"

"Yes. No! I—I'm privileged to meet you, Ms. Valdez."

She gave him a quick glance, then dropped her eyes to her work. "What kind of meat do you want?" she asked.

"I make the sausage myself," Vern announced.

Anita flashed the man a white-toothed grin and Jack was enchanted all over again.

"I'll take sausage, then," he said and eagerly readied his most-charming smile, but she piled sausage on a plate without sparing him another glance and sent the plate down the line to receive generous helpings of beans, potato salad and coleslaw. She continued dishing up meat for the crowd that pressed into the food tent.

"Have you seen Bill Wiatrek?" Vern asked Anita as he pointed at brisket. Jack recognized the school principal's name.

The vision gestured artistically with her tongs. "I think he's over playing horseshoes."

"Figures. Thanks, Anita. See ya later."

"Well, uh, it was nice to meet you," Jack said, reluctantly setting off after his plate.

As they left the tent with loaded plates and huge glasses of iced tea, Vern confided to Jack, "She's got a brother—senior this year. Think you ought to look into recruiting him."

"I'd be glad to—if... Well, you haven't offered me the job yet, sir," Jack said.

Vern flashed shrewd eyes his way. "Son, you think a town like ours would turn down someone with your credentials?"

The reference to his past was disheartening. Even in The-Back-of-Beyond, Texas, someone had heard of him. "I don't have any coaching experience." Jack felt obliged to point that out.

"And we don't have any assistant coaches or fancy training facilities and you have to teach two Texas history classes and one basic math in addition to your football duties," Vern retorted. "We haven't had a winning season in five years. Haven't been in the playoffs in twenty years."

"I can't guarantee a winning season," Jack protested. "I think the kids should enjoy themselves, learn self-discipline and master basic physical skills. That's more important at this point in their development than winning games."

"Sure, I agree. But you're a winner, Jack. They're bound to learn a winning attitude from you. It isn't often a small school like ours gets a chance to hire a man who set passing records in the Super Bowl."

Jack started to protest again— He'd only played that one year before being hurt. He stopped. This was the weirdest interview he'd ever had. Were they trying to convince each other of their unsuitability? The beautiful vision he'd just met still occupied a burning spot in his mind. "Is Anita—is she Mrs. or Miss Valdez?"

"It's Miss," Vern answered and grinned. "I think maybe we can do some business, Jack. What do you say? Want to coach the Larson Fighting Badgers?"

Jack took a deep breath. He'd spent those grueling months in rehabilitation putting not only his knee but his life back together. He'd figured out what he wanted and what he didn't. He didn't want to lead with his mouth again—blurt out something impulsive that would haunt him forever afterward. He did want stability, normalcy.

Jack looked around at the laughing families playing games and eating barbecue dinners, raising money for the volunteer fire department of a small American town on Independence Day.

Take it slow, buddy. Think. Investigate, he told himself as his head was nodding vigorously. "If it's okay with Mr. Wiatrek."

"Who do you think suggested you?"

Jack followed Vern to a long picnic table in the shade of a tree with feathery-looking foliage. As they ate and talked, the principal and the other school-board members drifted over and joined them. He only saw Anita once more from a distance, but the sun glinted on her black hair and outlined her feminine curves quite spectacularly.

By the time he left Larson to drive to San Antonio and catch his flight back to Los Angeles, Jack was officially signed, sealed and delivered: the Fighting Badgers's new football coach. He sat awkwardly through the plane ride, impatient to return to his apartment so he could pack up his belongings and prepare his resignation from the sporting goods store. He wanted to get back to Texas before somebody else scooped up Anita Valdez and carried her off.

No woman had ever made him feel all swirly inside like that. Had it really been Anita Valdez or was it the heat? More importantly—had she felt any of the same swirliness about him?

He had to get back to Larson and start finding out.

Chapter Two

Jesse was looking intently down the hallway. "He's here!" Jesse's hiss startled Anita out of her afternoon lethargy. What replaced it was worse. *Anticipation.* How could those few seconds create such a lingering impression?

"Who?" Anita knew darned well who. The person responsible for Jesse's only show of interest since the fire. From the minute the school board officially hired the bozo, her brother hadn't talked about anything else. After months of strained silence, they'd been arguing for weeks.

"The new football coach, Sis—geez, he looks like a movie star. You'd better get in line. The girls'll be fallin' all over themselves to get to him."

There was no way she'd admit she'd reacted that way when she'd glanced up at him at the picnic. She'd felt a silly roaring sensation, like being sucked into a tornado. Even now, weeks later, the memory of the man's masculinity, size and presence was fresh and overpowering.

"Let them." Between her responsibilities to her brother and her job duties, she had plenty to keep her busy. She had no business getting interested in anyone, let alone someone like *him*. And she wasn't interested—just . . . affected.

Jesse started to say something, then shrugged and asked artlessly, "Do you need me to take something down to the school office?"

"Like what?" Anita asked dryly. "A bandage for the copy machine?" In spite of her opposition to its source, Anita smiled at her brother's enthusiasm. It was good to see him interested in something again. Jesse had always been outgoing and effervescent. After their folks died, he'd built a wall around himself that Anita couldn't penetrate. She felt so helpless, watching him go silently through the motions of living, knowing he hurt, not being able to heal the wound.

She decided to encourage Jesse's positive behavior and ignore the trigger. "Why don't you sweep your way down the hall and maybe you can meet him?"

"Great idea, Sis!" The teenager vacated the office in record time, his steps fading as he raced down the empty hallway. Anita used the school clinic year-round. When she'd returned to Larson to take care of her brother, she'd accepted dual employment as school nurse/community health district officer. The halls would soon be packed: school started next week; football practice—as Jesse pointedly and frequently informed her—started tomorrow.

Thirty minutes later, as Anita shuffled reports into a neat pile, Jesse returned, bubbling with excitement. "He let me show him the whole school, 'Nita! And he called me Jesse and everything—he's really nice. And he's single. I asked."

"You didn't." One look told her he had. She shook her head but said nothing. She didn't want to destroy her brother's first favorable reaction to anything in months, but . . . Anita shrugged. Jesse was too young to understand. *If the man's so nice, why does he make a living endangering kids?*

"He asked me if I'm trying out for the team."

Ignoring her brother's challenging, sullen tone, Anita calmly picked up her purse and the reports and snapped off the office light. "I don't care what a great guy he is, Jesse, the answer's the same."

"Come on, Sis. Be reasonable."

Even as she vowed not to fight with him again, Anita snapped, "I'm doing what I think is best!"

"Yeah, right," Jesse grunted sullenly as he helped her carry the reports to her car. "You're just trying to run my life."

"That's my job, now. You're not playing football this year."

Anita was irritated enough at the new coach of the Larson High Fighting Badgers to forget the man who'd affected her so strongly in those few seconds at the Fourth of July picnic. She didn't remember his broad shoulders and hazel eyes and sexy grin. As Jesse's legal guardian, she was too busy to be interested in men of any kind and she refused to let her brother endanger his health or his future by playing a dangerous contact sport.

"I don't want you ending up like the Lopez boy. End of discussion." She ignored Jesse's muttering and headed for the car. By the time they dropped off the reports and reached their aunt and uncle's house, where they were living, Jesse had fallen silent and morose again.

Anita squeezed the steering wheel. Didn't he know how unsure of herself she felt? That she knew she could never replace their parents, but she had to try? "Jesse, please. I want you to be happy, but I'm supposed to take care of you. I have to do what I think is best. Please try to understand," Anita pleaded as she stopped the car.

He kept gazing out of the car window at the dry stalks in the cornfield behind their uncle's house. On the far side of that field were the charred remains of the house they'd grown up in. "Dad let me play last year," he said finally as he opened the passenger-side door to get out. Then he trudged into the house. Anita winced at the rebuke.

* * *

Jack ignored the sweat rolling down his back as he unloaded the car. It didn't hold much, but he hadn't accumulated much. So it ought to fit just fine in his new apartment. When he'd asked his new boss, Bill Wiatrek, about housing, he'd received directions here. Probably the only place in town.

There were four apartments in the "complex." One belonged to the older man who'd built them. If his luck had changed, Anita would live next door. No chance: the other two units were occupied by retirees.

Maybe she was only visiting for the holiday, he thought and dumped the last box in the tiny living room. He realized he should have asked the boy who'd shown him around school. Larson was so small, he probably knew who she was.

Jack focused on his new career to force his mind off his lingering sense of disappointment. The boy had been pretty nice. Said he'd played tailback last year. That was silly—long and lean like that, he was born to be a pass receiver....

Two days later, Jack swiped a glob of shaving cream from his palm and spread the lather over his stubbled cheeks. He ignored the morning pain in his knee and contorted his body into the already-familiar shape that allowed him to see his reflection in the tiny mirror. He began to scrape the whiskers off his face. Tiny mirror, tiny bathroom, tiny apartment, tiny town.

Too tiny for his purposes, but he had nobody to blame but himself.

Jack sighed and held the razor under a thin stream of water to rinse it off. He still hadn't seen Anita, although when he'd gone to Smolik's for lunch yesterday and tried to casually ask about her, Vern had laughed and made some crack about breaking a leg. Confused, Jack had dropped the subject.

A splash of after-shave slapped Jack's cheeks smartly. *Maybe it was just nerves about the interview or disap-*

pointment over the size of Larson that made her seem so wonderful. Maybe her hair wasn't lush, her eyes dark and romantic. Jack pulled on a T-shirt and stuffed the tail into his warm-up pants. He sat down to pull on socks and athletic shoes. *If we met again, I might wonder what I saw in her.*

The possibility didn't still the powerful need that gripped him. Jack closed his eyes against it. It was natural to want a wife, a family, a woman to love, honor and cherish, but when you'd believed your own publicity and thought you had a right to act like a first-class jerk, you had to pay for it.

A year of isolation in Larson, Texas, seemed appropriate, even though acceptance didn't make it easier.

Jack picked up a water jug, his clipboard and a whistle on a nylon cord and reminded himself that every coin had two sides. If Anita Valdez did live in Larson, sooner or later, they'd meet. She must be the only single woman in town. He was probably the only bachelor. With no competition, maybe he'd get a chance at that family, after all.

A few hours later, Jack paused and glanced up at the huge bleachers casting long shadows over the football field. Texas optimism, he decided. Probably never more than half-filled. "Okay, Group One, wind sprints. Group Two, agility drill—run through the tires. Group Three, zigzag thirty yards backward."

Out of the corner of his eye, Jack could see the kid who'd toured him around the school when he arrived. The boy was watching practice intently from the bleachers but made no move to join them. He'd said he wanted to play.... Jack made a mental note to ask someone what the deal was.

Two days of practice were too few to reach any real conclusions, but Jack was pleased with the caliber of the boys who'd turned out for the team. There was a goodly number of large stocky kids, some thin fast ones and enough bodies so that only a few would have to play both offense and defense. That was a blessing in this heat. Jack took his attention off the field long enough to locate the water jug. He'd advised the boys to be careful of dehydration; he ought to take his own advice.

"Ungh!" The normal adolescent chatter was silenced by a grunt of pain. Jack was moving toward the grunter before the crumpling boy hit the ground.

Please don't let it be broken, Jack prayed as he reached the boy, who'd caught his ankle in a tire and tripped. "It's okay, it's okay. Don't get up yet," he cautioned the boy, who shrugged off Jack's assistance and struggled to his feet with a pithy remark.

"Damn, Coach! Sh—"

"That's enough, son," Jack cut in quickly. "There's no need to prove your manliness with a gutter vocabulary." He addressed the boys clustered around them. "Anyone know what to do in these cases? Is there a doctor in town? How far away is the nearest hospital?"

"We can take him to the clinic, my sister'll be able to tell if we need to take him to Kenedy for X rays." It was the youngster from the bleachers, suddenly in the thick of the group crowding around the injured player.

"Kenedy's the nearest town with a hospital," the boy explained. "The clinic's right there—" He indicated a corner of the school.

"Okay, that's a good idea. Let's get you in there, uh—Bubba, right?" Jack was still sorting out kids by position—names, never his strong suit, were following slowly.

"Yes, sir." Bubba hopped toward the building with the help of two of the larger boys. Jack followed with Jesse.

"Did you really play professional football?"

"One year, that's all." It was best forgotten. His on-field activities had been outstanding, but his off-field life—years of hard-won wisdom later, Jack cringed at what his hotshot younger self had considered sophisticated behavior. "Your sister's the...school nurse?"

"Yes, sir." Jesse grinned, white teeth flashing against his bronze skin. "Also the community health district officer, also one of two EMTs for the county, also the midwife."

Jack added another inch of imagined height for every title—and another layer of stern, martial demeanor.

"What grade are you, Jesse?" Jack asked, abruptly changing the subject. He didn't want to think about a tough-as-nails master sergeant chewing him out for negligence. Although he couldn't figure out exactly how he could be held responsible for the clumsiness of big, growing kids like Bubba.

"I'm a senior this year, sir."

"Didn't you tell me you played last year?"

Like that, the kid's brightness faded. "Yeah."

Jack frowned. What had he said to upset the boy? "So why don't you come out this year? We could use you if you're as fast as you look."

Jack looked over at Jesse when the silence lengthened. At last, he got a reply.

"It's a sore subject, Coach. My parents—" The boy's jaw trembled slightly. "My parents are dead. My sister won't let me play. I want to, but—" Jesse's shrug expressed his anger and frustration eloquently. "When Sis gets an idea in her head, it takes dynamite to get it out!"

Jack nodded sympathetically, mentally preparing himself for the worst. An amazon with a Doberman's temperament. *You're in for it now, Hayden.*

They entered the deserted school and Jesse pointed to a door whose upper half was glass. A sign on the glass identified it as the Larson Health District Office and School Clinic. Jack and Jesse passed through an empty waiting room-office combination; voices came from the back room, which Jesse explained was the clinic proper. Jack stopped in the clinic doorway.

"Are you sure it doesn't hurt when I rotate it this way?" The question, directed at Bubba, was soft and full of concern. It was asked by an achingly familiar petite being—the woman Jack had been dreaming about for the past six weeks. Except that she was even lovelier than he remembered. Jesse's sister was Anita Valdez, the most enticing, beautiful, intriguing woman in the world.

A delicate scent of spring flowers mingled with the smell of rubbing alcohol and bandages. Her perfume. Jack inhaled deeply, then all he could do was stare at the tiny, feminine apparition in a pale blue uniform blouse and pants—and experience a falling sensation while his stomach did cartwheels.

"How's Bubba?" Jesse asked.

"Fine," Anita answered firmly, ridiculously proud of maintaining her professional attitude despite the electricity crackling from the hunk filling the doorway. "It's just sprained, I think. Charlie, run across to the Dairy Queen and get some extra ice. Is this—?" She hadn't wanted to ask, but she might as well hear it from the horse's mouth. Just to set the record straight. Hunk or not, he was the enemy.

"Oh, sorry! Sis, this is Coach Hayden. Coach, my sister, Anita Valdez."

"Anita." He said her name so slowly, it sounded like a foreign word. Maybe to him it was. "I don't know if you remember," he went on in a smooth, deep voice, "but we met briefly at the volunteer firemen's Fourth of July picnic."

Anita didn't answer immediately. For some crazy reason, her composure had deserted her. At last, she managed a cool nod of greeting, but she certainly was too smart to admit she remembered him.

"Mr. Hayden. You're Hollywood Hayden, aren't you?" she heard herself ask and almost groaned. That was worse than admitting she recalled meeting him!

"Y-yes, ma'am. Well, I played there. My dad's retired now, but he was career air force, so I've lived all over. Never in a town this small, though. You must even have to import crime!" He cleared his throat awkwardly. "Anyway, I'm the, uh, new football coach. I'll also be teaching math and history. And my name's Jack," he added in a rush, as though he'd just remembered.

Probably hit by too many tackles. Anita busied herself wrapping Bubba's ankle, then preparing an ice pack when

Charlie got back with the ice. It wasn't easy ignoring the man— He seemed to give off waves of energy, filling the air and her insides with strange magnetic pulses. Anita kept her eyes riveted on Bubba's ankle.

The women in this county and the next are going to fight over Jack Hayden like vultures on road kill, Anita thought. *His sophistication outclasses anything in Larson, even though his intelligence is apparently the equivalent of a dead skunk's.* As she worked, he ventured one or two inane questions, which Jesse answered. Anita finally risked another glance at the man through her lashes. Yes, with a body like that—hard and muscular, broad-shouldered and narrow-hipped—not to mention his warm hazel eyes and a grin that was somehow sexy and cute at the same time...

With his looks, this guy doesn't need any brains, she mused, then pulled herself up short. This man was in charge of that dangerous sport that Jesse wanted to play—and she'd better remember it. "There you go, Bubba. Keep it elevated and iced the rest of the day, then see how it is in the morning. If it's still swollen, you'd better get some X rays."

"Thanks, Ms. Valdez." Bubba and the other boys suddenly vacated the clinic with a clatter of cleats.

Anita rolled up her tape and put away her scissors. Hayden was still standing there, looking at her. "Was there anything else?" Why, the man hadn't moved an inch! "Is there a problem, Mr. Hayden?"

He started from his stupor. "Uh, no, no—it's Miss Valdez, isn't it?" He was tense, waiting for her answer, apparently with bated breath.

"Well, if you want to be technical. Valdez—same surname as my brother, get it?" Under normal circumstances, she'd never use such cool tones and clipped words, but Jack Hayden was a threat.

Not a personal one, of course, but Jesse didn't understand how dangerous contact sports are. And Anita did.

A rotation through a rehab unit during nursing school had taught her that. And Marco Lopez, the Larson student—how could she possibly allow her brother to risk the injury the Lopez boy had suffered last year?

Anita dropped the roll of gauze, bent to pick it up. When she straightened, Hayden was still standing there, goldy-green eyes boring deep into her. Sudden heat rose in her to rival the August sun. This man was definitely disruptive—in more ways than one! "What *are* you staring at?" she cried out in exasperation.

"You. I've... I've never seen anyone... like you before."

He sounded like someone in a trance, for heaven's sake. What was wrong with the man? "What do you mean? You've never seen a Hispanic before?"

Her sharp question must have pierced his fog at last because Hayden roused himself enough to put a look of bewilderment on his face. "Hispanic? Oh. Sure, but I've never seen a woman as incredibly beautiful as you. I think I've been looking for you everywhere, my whole life, only I didn't know it was you. I—" He flushed, as if finally registering her glowering reaction. "I'm sorry, I didn't mean... That is, I'm not—"

If Jack Hayden thought his electricity and his adolescent, amateurish compliments could turn her head enough to change her mind, he was mistaken. She knew, medically and psychologically, what happened to paralytics.

And she knew that accidents happened. She'd lost her parents; she was solely responsible for her brother. She shouldn't have so much trouble remembering those facts just because of a set of magnificent shoulders and a bedroom smile. After all, a few dates with a surgical resident had taught her that the inner man didn't always match the outer image.

"Save your breath, mister." Anita dropped the gauze into a drawer and slammed it shut. "I'm not interested."

"In what?" At last, he looked completely alert.

"In letting my brother play ball for you."

"I thought I said you were beautiful— What does that have to do with Jesse? It would help him, though. I know when my mom died, I—" He swallowed.

She held up a hand, palm outward. "I know what you're doing."

"Do you?" he growled softly, sending shivers up Anita's spine. "I was stating a fact about you. Your brother's interest in joining the team is another subject." He seemed to miss the connection. "Will you go out with me tonight?"

Anita stared up at the man facing her. He was at least a foot taller than her own five-foot-two frame. Jesse was both right and wrong with his movie-star remark, she thought as she studied Jack's face. Hayden wasn't exactly handsome—his features were too ruggedly masculine and his nose was too crooked to fit that description, but there was something dangerously, disarmingly charming about him. Oh, yes, Jack Hayden was undeniably attractive. He awaited her answer with one eyebrow raised almost to his short, thick brown hair. It looked as soft as mink.... Anita cut off her drifting thoughts.

"No!"

"Why not?"

Anita blinked. When Hayden was hired, the local newspaper had run a photo of him from his playing days. Anita wondered if this was the same man. There was more character in his face now, less cockiness in his smile, but these idiotic questions matched the old Hollywood image. Couldn't the man take no for an answer?

"Look, Mr. Hayden, I don't mean to be rude, but I'm... unavailable."

"Does that mean you're involved with someone?" A tiny vertical furrow appeared between his big, beautiful eyes.

"No. It means I'm uninterested." *Oh, Anita—you liar!* "I'm not interested in someone who sweet-talks every woman he meets just for practice!"

"I don't need any practice," he began, then frowned.

"No, your delivery was real smooth—but it was still a line, if I ever heard one."

"Whoa, as I believe you say in Texas," Jack said with a grin and an uplifted palm. "It wasn't a line. It was the plain truth. Honest."

"Talk is cheap, Mr. Hayden."

Jack's smile was oddly touching, almost bittersweet, as he shook his head slowly. "No, Anita, you're wrong," he said softly. "Talk can be very costly, sometimes. It cost me a chance at happiness once. At least I thought I'd be happy enough...."

She ignored his reference, but for one second, Anita felt a flicker of empathy for this huge male with the expressive eyes and aura of quiet strength. Deliberately, she asked, "Did you learn your non-line in the NFL?"

Suddenly, his face was all harsh angles, but his voice sounded tired. "I never needed any. Women came to me. They'd wait outside the locker room, in the hotel lobbies, everywhere. In droves, Ms. Valdez. I didn't have to be glib, I just had to be available."

She didn't mean to ask. "Were you?"

He shrugged, but didn't smile. She had no business remembering how charming his smile was. "More than I should have been, though I was more selective than most." He shrugged again. "But that's in the past. I learned my lesson."

Me, too, she thought, *and I'm not about to unlearn it at the first tingle that comes along. I'm responsible for my brother's safety and Jack Hayden is a threat to it. A very attractive, seductive threat.* A flash of panic raced through her; in self-defense she turned it to anger.

Jack felt the heat as her dark eyes flashed, observed the dangerous tilt of her chin. He knew when it was time to retreat. "Well, it was nice to see you again, Ms. Valdez. Thanks for looking at Bubba's ankle. Bye!" As he spoke, he inched rapidly backward until he reached the clinic's outer door. There, he turned and fled with as much dignity as he could manage while limping to the nearest exit.

Darned knee, he thought, though he knew he was lucky he was even mobile enough to limp. The doctors who put it back together hadn't been sure he would ever walk unaided again, but his physical therapist had insisted. Some days now, it was almost pain free. Other days, he gritted his teeth and made the aspirin companies wealthy.

Returning to practice, Jack put the team back to work learning two plays he diagrammed for them. They were sharp kids, quick on the uptake, he saw with satisfaction. He managed to finish the session without major instructional mistakes, but his mind was definitely not on football. It was on the beautiful woman he'd seen in the school clinic and her unmistakable antagonism—even before he'd made those idiotic remarks about his prowess with women. Why couldn't he open his mouth without putting his foot into it? Had he ruined his chances before he even got started?

In the hot dry air, Jack felt a chill. He gathered his equipment as he shrugged off the feeling.

Anita didn't want her brother to play football. Okay, it was a stumbling block to their relationship, but it could be resolved. He'd hate to give up any help he could get for the team, of course, but he wasn't about to give up what this woman made him feel. Not without further exploration.

"Jesse!" The boy was sliding off the bleachers and ambling away with that loose-gaited adolescent walk that Jack's experienced eye could translate as speed and potential grace. "Jesse, wait!"

Jack had one foot planted on the first step of the unpainted porch. He nervously adjusted his collar. He'd raced home from practice and showered, then had chosen his outfit: navy cotton slacks, Italian leather slip-ons with tassels, a braided leather belt and a silk shirt. It was all slightly outdated and too flashy for his current life-style, but he hadn't had a lot of extra money since his playing days and he'd had plenty of expenses. Nothing left over for clothes, but Jesse had assured him Anita would be impressed. *Like she was this afternoon?* Jack wondered ruefully. "Are you sure your aunt and uncle won't mind?"

"I'm sure. Come on, I'll introduce you." Jesse was already through the door of the small wood-frame house, which was a couple of miles outside Larson. Jack glanced back once at his car—he'd parked it out of the way beside an ancient tractor on the grass.

When he'd hailed Jesse after practice, he'd tried to gently pump the boy about his sister and her objections to Jack Hayden and football—and been immediately invited for dinner. It was nice to have one Valdez cooperating with him. Now if only a certain female Valdez would do the same....

Jesse's brief explanation of the living arrangements had given Jack food for thought. Seventeen was young to face the loss of your parents. Jack felt even more strongly now that Jesse would benefit from participating in an extracurricular sport.

Inside the modest home, Jack was introduced to Jesse's aunt and uncle, who spoke almost no English but managed to make him feel welcome. After politely shaking hands with Uncle Juan and Aunt Isabel, he met their children, a boy of twelve and a girl of seven.

Smiling at the little girl who peeked at him from behind Jesse's legs, Jack thought he sounded very casual when he said, "Please tell your aunt and uncle it's really nice of them to invite me for dinner. I haven't quite mastered the gas stove in my apartment yet— Is Anita going to be here?"

Jesse grinned at the coach. "Yeah," the boy drawled. "She oughta be back in time for supper."

Jack bit back a relieved grin. He hadn't had any luck with romantic relationships since his days as Hollywood Hayden. Apparently plain Jack wasn't very appealing. The one possible relationship had heard about his past and dumped him pronto. Not that she'd ever made him feel the way Anita did already.

Jack stuck his hands in his pockets to hide his nerves. He wanted Anita to give him a chance, but he had no lures, no powers of persuasion. Only hope and a willing spirit. He hoped it would be enough.

Chapter Three

With a sigh of relief, Anita turned into Uncle Juan's gravel driveway. It had been a long day, ending with the summons that sent her racing from the clinic. *Hope Jesse got a ride home.*

Luckily, it was a false alarm. Anita didn't blame Janie for calling, though—she'd have done it herself if her baby had fallen from a second-story window. Even into a nice fat bush.

For one slow second, Anita couldn't smother the wave of longing for a child of her own. Well, she had parental responsibilities now, even if they weren't exactly what she'd envisioned. When she'd received the devastating news about her parents, she'd given up her dumb love-and-marriage dreams and come home to take care of Jesse.

It was just too bad that the one man who ever made her tremble turned out to be engaged in a repugnant occupation. And admitted to a positively hectic social history.

Anita parked, then strolled across the yard inhaling the refreshing scent of plowed earth and clean air. There was an oddly familiar-looking strange car sitting next to her uncle's old tractor. A warning tingle shot through her. *Oh, no...!* Anita took the steps two at a time.

Jack tried to keep his feet tucked under his chair and his wits about him. Neither task was easy. He was six foot three and his rebuilt knee really didn't like being completely bent, but the table was crowded and Jack wanted to keep his big feet out of everyone's way.

As to keeping his wits—impossible. Anita was sitting directly opposite him and every time he looked up from his plate of rice with pork and *calabasita,* he looked into her beautiful oval face. Saw her dark exotic eyes, her curving lips, her smooth skin, her... "Excuse me?"

"Petey wants to know if you ever met Earl Campbell," Jesse said.

For a moment, Jack stared at the shyly smiling younger boy, unable to remember who Earl Campbell was. *Oh.* "Sure. Met him at an awards banquet in Detroit. Or was it the one in Denver? Anyway—he's pretty famous in Texas, huh?"

Like trained seals, Jack's eyes and his attention returned to Anita. He couldn't help it—he'd spent those long months in rehab regaining his sanity along with the use of his knee. He positively yearned for normalcy and all its trappings. Although his wild-oats past kept rearing its ugly head until—even before...Miranda, that was her name—he'd given up on love, Jack had clung stubbornly to the hope of finding someone willing to give him a chance to be a devoted husband and father.

He'd never imagined he'd be lucky enough to fall headlong, deep-water, full-bore infatuated with such a beautiful woman. In Larson, Texas, of all places. Now he had one goal: to convince the object of his interest to return the favor.

The first step was to get her to speak to him. She hadn't said one word since she'd charged into the house and said, "You!"

She'd given him a single blistering look before disappearing into the kitchen. At the table, she helped the younger children fill their plates, and now was getting up to answer the telephone.

You've got to do something, Jack, he told himself. The boys were asking too many of the wrong questions. The more they dug up the past, the more Anita simmered.

"I've got to go again," Anita said, first in Spanish, then in English. "Lynette Pawelek is in labor."

Jack was on his feet, gripping the table for support, before she finished the sentence. "I'll take you."

"I have a car," she said.

"Well, yes, but—well, maybe I could ride along." He tried for a friendly smile, wondering if he'd have to chain himself to her bumper. "Perhaps you could show me the rest of the town on the way. I've been so busy with practices—" He choked to a halt. He'd done it again! He'd sworn he wasn't going to mention football, since it upset her, and there he went, bringing it up!

"There isn't much to see of Larson except the road out of here." Her steady gaze spoke volumes, but Jack's heart was beating too loudly to hear them.

Jesse had been translating softly into Spanish; now his uncle said something to Anita, who nodded reluctantly. "Tío Juan reminds me to be hospitable, so let's go."

"I won't faint," he assured her as they walked to her car.

"I don't care if you do—as long as you stay out of my way." *And out of my mind.* It had been three hours since their meeting over Bubba's ankle and Anita hadn't been able to shake Jack Hayden's effect. His magnetism would sneak up on her at odd moments, bringing little shivers of— *Oh, shoot. This is ridiculous.* They got into the car and Anita started down the driveway.

"You don't like me, do you?" The sorrow in his tone was unmistakable. For a second, Anita heard something else in his deep voice, too. Something hot and compelling.

In self-preservation, she tried to play dumb. "What do you mean?"

"Look, I'm sorry for blurting that out this afternoon—about your being so beautiful. I thought most women like sincere compliments. I guess you don't. At least not from me."

He could certainly sound sincere. Anita took her eyes off the road long enough to be hooked by his lost-puppy look. *Oh, for heaven's sake,* she lectured herself. *Falling for goo-goo eyes, no matter how well done, is inexcusable.* "That's not it." Why, the words had come out almost apologetically! What was he doing to her?

"It wasn't a line. Really, Anita. You're convicting me without a trial," he said and sighed. He was making her feel sorry for him!

"Jack—"

"That's the first time you've said my name." He sounded positively thrilled.

"It'll be the last if you don't shut up and listen to me." He was grinning at her; she was so busy suppressing a giggle and trying to remember how long it had been since she'd had that impulse, she almost forgot what she intended to say. This man must have a patent on his tingle-creation trick. *He's just trying to soften you up,* she warned herself. *You've got to think about Jesse's welfare.* And her own. Hollywood Hayden... She didn't dare lose her heart to the wrong man. She didn't need any more pain.

Yet somehow, she just couldn't make herself tell him to get lost. "Mr. Hayden, I'm sure you're a very nice person...."

"But—" he prompted when she hesitated. "You have some strong objections to me."

"To football. I won't have my brother playing it. Period."

Jack grinned winsomely. "Anita, once you get to know me, you might like me. Let's see—I have a younger sister. Maddie was an Olympic ski team alternate. She married a music librarian, for gosh sakes, and is deliriously happy.

"As for football—can't we separate the two? I mean, sure I'd like Jesse on the team. It would be mutually beneficial, but... Let me take you to dinner and we can discuss your objections."

That was suave. *The man has the market cornered when it comes to charm, but I'm immune. It's only smart to be cautious, isn't it?* "I'm trying to tell you—" Anita stopped the car in front of a neat, well-kept house trailer. Jack put his hand over hers. The warmth of his touch sent little tremors coursing through her. Geez, was she so lonely that one touch and longing eyes could sidetrack her devotion to being an overnight parenting success?

"I don't think I want to hear what you're trying to tell me, Anita." There was a gleam of panic in his expressive eyes.

"I'm telling you... I'm not going to dinner with you." That wasn't what she meant to say! She meant to tell him in no uncertain terms to leave her and her brother alone. Anita ran her free hand over her hair. What was wrong with her?

The gleam turned to satisfaction—and something hard-edged: determination. Her tingles grew stronger, hotter.

His eyes are such a soft green in the long evening light, she thought dreamily.

"Can't we be friends, Anita? We'll be working closely together at school. We should cooperate."

She wanted to cooperate his mouth with hers. Her eyes widened at the spontaneous urge. She grabbed her black bag. "Wait out here," she ordered as she raced up the steps of the trailer. Without looking back, she went inside. He heard a low murmur of voices that gradually faded.

Left alone, Jack helped himself to a lawn chair under a canopy extending from the trailer, and studied his surroundings. A far cry from the cities he'd lived in. No traffic, no sirens, no subliminal machinery hum to disturb the twilight peace. The only sound was a light wind sifting through the low, bent trees that edged long fields of pale yellow stubble. He could see part of a house peeking out from a wooded area in the distance. Cicadas began their long evening chorus.

"Kinda nice, this time o'day, ain't it?"

Jack jumped at the unexpected sound, then stood carefully and stuck out his hand to the speaker: a youngish man wearing a baseball cap and a nervous grin. He was almost as tall as Jack and heftier, and there was something vaguely familiar about him.

"Yes, it is. Not as hot, that's for sure. I'm Jack Hayden."

"Figured you was. Dale Pawelek." They shook hands, then Dale tipped his head toward the half-hidden house. "That's m'folks place. Think you know my brother Danny and our cousin Greg."

"Greg Pawelek, sure—my big offensive guard. Danny's my quarterback. Great arm— He's your brother?"

The man grinned. "One of 'em. There's six of us boys. Two girls. Want something to drink?"

"Well, a soda would taste good."

Dale disappeared inside the trailer, returning shortly with two cans. He handed one over. "Only flavor we got—the wife likes this kind...." He took off his cap and wiped his forehead with the back of his hand.

"It's fine," Jack assured him and opened it. He gestured with the sweat-beaded can toward the trailer and the event taking place as they talked. "Is... this your first?"

"Yeah." The answer sighed out of him. Jack could see the young man was wound tight and trying not to show it. He felt a bond of sympathy join his initial jolt of envy. He searched for something comforting and safe to say.

"I'm sure everything will be fine. Ms. Valdez seems quite competent."

For once, he'd said the right thing. Relief was plain on Dale's sunburned face. "Yeah, she sure is. Lucky for us she came back from San Antonio... though it was a terrible thing, her and Jesse losin' their folks in that fire. They were asleep—that's a small blessing. And Jesse was spendin' the night with Danny."

"They seem to be handling it pretty well." He'd observed so many examples of the strength and courage of ordinary people during his physical therapy stint.

"Well as can be expected, I guess. Danny's worried about Jesse, though. Jesse's sharp, but...even Danny says he needs motivatin'. He gonna play this year?"

At Jack's frown, the soon-to-be father grinned knowingly. "She won't let him, right?"

Jack nodded. "It'd be good for the boy—keep him too busy to brood."

"But I don't guess 'Nita sees it that way," Dale said. "You hear about Marco Lopez?"

Dread settled in the pit of Jack's stomach. There *was* someone else! "M-Marco Lopez?" he croaked out.

Dale shot him a glance. "Kid on last year's team. Wasn't in great shape to start with. Took a bad hit. Paralyzed him from the waist down." He jerked a thumb in the direction of the trailer. "That plus losin' her folks—she won't even think of lettin' Jesse play."

It was as if he'd been looking through a kaleidoscope. Dale had just given the end a twist and a whole new picture fell into place. *So it's not me she doesn't like, it's football.* He didn't know whether to be discouraged or energized by the challenge.

"I think you're right—playin' would help," the prospective father ventured as they studied the empty fields together. "But I don't imagine 'Nita feels that way."

"Probably not," Jack agreed. "The team could use him if he's as fast as I think he is, but..." His head was spinning. The situation was like an option offense with a kazillion options. If he accepted Anita's objections to Jesse's playing, maybe she'd give him a chance personally. But Jesse—Jack agreed with Dale. The boy needed what organized sports could give him during this difficult period of adjustment.

"What do you think of our chances this year?" When Jack looked blank, Dale prompted him. "In football!"

"Oh!" Jack mentally switched gears, an effort he wouldn't have had to make a few years ago. Funny how a life-changing injury alters a person's perspective on what's important. He had that in common with Anita. It was a start—that and the way she made his heart thump. "I think we'll have some fun. The guys are enthusiastic, better conditioned than I expected...."

"Dale, come on in now." Anita's request as it came from the top step of the trailer had a river of joy in it Jack hadn't heard before. What if someday she spoke to *him* with that river in her voice?

Jack's falling sensation grew stronger.

Dale rushed into the trailer. Anita came slowly down the steps, stretching her arms above her head. Jack tried not to ogle her exquisite curves. He wasn't particularly successful, but he was lucky: Anita didn't notice.

"Is it—"

"A very healthy nine-pound boy."

"Wow. That's big for a first baby." Once upon a time, in a fit of misplaced optimism, he'd learned a lot about the subject. Maybe, if he was very, very careful now, the effort wouldn't be wasted.

"Paweleks tend to have large babies." Anita rubbed her face slowly.

Jack guided her to the lawn chair. As she sank into it with a sigh, he said, "Larson's lucky to have you, since it can't support one doctor. I supported several single-handledly," he mused with a chuckle, then after an awkward pause, added, "It must be nice to know your patients so well." It was halfway a question.

Too tired to defend her hometown, Anita said, "After nursing school, I worked in a hospital in San Antonio, took my EMT training there. It's exciting but—your patients are strangers and they stay that way." *I came home because I had to—but I'd missed Larson all along. I like knowing every name and every face. It's like having a huge extended family.*

"People don't stay strangers here." That one sounded almost like praise. Anita felt confused. One minute, Jack pointed out Larson's shortcomings, the next he seemed to like the place. Jack wasn't fitting her preconceived notions, but...

That resident had done a good job of opening her eyes to her own naiveté. Now she had to keep them open.

"I know everybody in the county," she said finally, "and they know me. We tend one another's business, too." She tried to make it sound like a vaguely sinister warning instead of civic pride.

"I'll keep that in mind, Anita." His rich voice caressed her across the growing darkness. Then it was right above her, moving downward. "I'll be very discreet."

His mouth descended on hers before she could think, prepare, move. His kiss was warm and firm and sizzling with intimate promises and desire. His arms were around her, gently but inexorably lifting her from the lawn chair, drawing her closer. That was exactly the way she wanted him: closer. One of them made a low noise deep in the throat, then...

"Want to see my new son, Coach?"

They sprang apart at the proud father's query. His bulk filled the doorway of the trailer; the light spilling from it didn't reach far enough to illuminate them.

"Sure, sure I would," Jack said shakily and stepped forward, giving Anita time to smooth her hair down and slow her—he hoped—racing pulse. His was still going light speed.

"Have you picked out a name yet?"

"Augustus Dale Pawelek the Third," Dale declared proudly, handing over the blue-blanketed infant for Jack's inspection.

Jack peered at the sleeping bundle. "He's beautiful," he breathed. "Look, Anita," he said, staring at the baby in utter fascination. "Isn't he the most incredible, most wonderful thing you've ever seen?"

* * *

"You really meant that back there, didn't you?" Anita asked a half hour later as the Pawelek trailer disappeared behind her taillights. "About that baby's being wonderful."

She felt rather than saw one massive shoulder lift and drop, heard a man trying to make light of his display of tenderness. "Well, I...I never held a newborn baby before. It's pretty awesome."

"Yes, it is." Anita tried to make conversation destroy the hot thread of desire his kiss had left burning in her heart. "Although I'll bet it wears a little thin at three o'clock in the morning."

She drove down her uncle's driveway and stopped in front of the sleeping house.

"I suppose so," he agreed doubtfully. "Thanks for letting me go along, though. It was an amazing experience." They both knew he wasn't talking about babies any longer.

"Here's your car. It's late—you should go home." Night sounds filled the silence between them. When his head moved toward her, she lifted a hand quickly. "No. It was an accident. Not repeatable. Go home."

Jack fumbled for the door handle. "That kiss was no accident, Anita. Thank your aunt for dinner. About Jesse..."

The inside light went on as he opened the car door; he was wearing his puppy-dog look—and darned if she didn't hear herself saying, "Well, I guess he could do those practice drills—the exercise would be good for him. But—"

"But no contact stuff, right?"

"Right." She couldn't believe she was giving Jesse permission for even limited participation, but this man was lethal to a woman's willpower. Well, a trip tomorrow to replace the flowers on her parents' grave would rebuild her resolve.

* * *

It did. And yet, when she marched out Friday afternoon to insist that Jesse stop running those snaking patterns across the field while Danny launched the ball in a long arc in his direction . . .

She stood on the grassy sidelines and watched Jesse laughing and shouting playful boasts with Danny and the others. Seeing her brother's joy after all the months of sorrow was like catching a glimpse of sunlight on a dreary overcast day.

As she turned and started to leave, a rich warm voice hailed her. "Anita!"

He said her name so joyfully! Her shivery response was only relief, though. Or maybe a little pleasure at the novelty of it. Jesse usually pronounced her name in anger or disgust. And most of her clients were either in pain or scared or both.

Jack loped over to her, leaving the boys to flop down in the long shadows of the afternoon. "Anita, hi! Long time no see."

She looked up at his tingle-producing smile and tried feebly to fight its effect. "I can see it's your sex appeal that attracted the ladies' attention in Hollywood, not your sparkling repartee," she said before she could stop herself. Jack Hayden was hell on inhibitions!

"Huh?" His smile faltered a little and she felt terrible. She was opposed to this man's occupation and she didn't have time for a schoolgirl crush on a certified hunk, but she didn't have to be rude.

Before she could apologize or remove Jesse from the team or any of the six other things she thought about doing, Jack said quietly, "If you're referring to the wannabe starlets I dated while I played for Los Angeles, what got their attention was the chance for some free publicity."

"Jack, I—"

"Those days are over." It was gentle but firm.

Are they? For how long? she wondered as she watched his features change from warm and inviting to hard and stony and back again. Who exactly was Jack Hayden? The mystery was just one more thing about the man that kept Anita in the center of a whirlwind.

"I don't have tornado insurance," she muttered.

Jack didn't understand her comment, so he ignored it. "I'd still like to take you out to dinner this weekend. I'm not big on Dairy Queen, but if there's no alternative, I can handle it."

She was shaking her head. "I'm busy."

"All weekend? Sorry, Anita," he added quickly, sheepishly. "It's none of my business."

"I'm taking a refresher course in Corpus Christi Saturday." She raised a hand to forestall any more tempting offers. "There isn't a French restaurant within fifty miles, anyway."

"Actually, I'm more partial to sushi. Anita—one of these days, let's discuss false perceptions."

Anita was confused. Again.

"However, I can take a hint if bludgeoned with it." Jack's smile was wistful. "I'll see you at school Tuesday." He turned away.

"Are the Larson Labor Day festivities beneath you?"

He spun around so fast, he stumbled. He put a hand on her shoulder to steady himself and she revised her estimation of his cleverness. *Slick move, Hollywood. And effective. One touch and my heart's racing like the wind.*

"Not if you go with me, Ms. Valdez!" Before she could produce a disclaimer, he said, "I'll pick you up—when?"

The eager grin lighting his face silenced her first instinctive denial. She refused to name the impulse behind her invitation—it must be nothing more than pure Texas hospitality. "Eleven o'clock. You have to get there early or the barbecue's gone."

"Don't worry. I know one of the servers."

"Not this time, mister. This time, I'm playing, not working."

Jack grinned again. "Even better, my dear." He twirled an invisible mustache. "See you Monday at eleven."

* * *

Anita jerked forward on the seat as Jack braked too hard. She readjusted the seat belt and looked at him. "What's the matter, Hayden?" she asked with a slight smile. "Never driven in traffic before?"

"I used to drive L.A.'s rush hour with my eyes closed," he assured her. "I just can't get over how the population of Larson mushrooms for holiday picnics. Must be the most exciting events of the year around here. Where do all these people come from?" He gestured at the throngs of people surging toward the food tent.

Anita tried to glare at him, but who could look at that profile without getting kind of breathless and forgetful? "Look, I know Larson's a small town and you're from a big city—"

"Several big cities," Jack corrected.

Anita ignored his interruption. "But your put-downs are uncalled-for."

"I wasn't putting anyone down," he insisted with the apparent earnestness of a ten-year-old. "I was expressing amazement, that's all. The turnout is fantastic."

"A lot of folks come in from the country," she explained and closed her eyes. She wanted to remember her latest game plan: expose Larson's female population to Jack Hayden and vice versa. While he was occupied with them, she might gather enough willpower to insist that Jesse choose some safe recreational activity. Like flower-arranging.

"Apparently so." He fell silent as he eased his low-slung sports car over the ruts in the field where they were directed to park. "I like it when you call me Jack," he said as he shut off the engine.

She looked at him and one corner of her mouth rose. "You do it so well, but—aren't you a little sophisticated to be acting coy?"

His smile answered hers. "Is that what I'm doing?"

"Well, you're up to something, Hayden," Anita insisted, fighting down a laugh.

"Don't you believe in innocent until proven guilty?"

Anita's lightheartedness faded. "In your case, I don't dare."

"What do you mean, you don't dare?" The question was too intense to avoid. A crowd streamed past the car; they ignored it.

"I know what you want and I think you'll stop at nothing to get it."

She hoped he couldn't hear any of her fear. After the traumas of recent months, Anita knew she was emotionally fragile—and Jack Hayden had a powerful effect on her.

"And what exactly do I want?"

The wide firm shoulders, the soft kind eyes and the deep warm voice led Anita's gaze to his mouth. It had been such a short kiss—but so intoxicating! "I know what you want." Her repetition sounded drugged rather than insistent.

Jack leaned toward her; a passing cowboy slapped the hood of the car and grinned at the startled couple.

"I think what we want right now better be barbecue, Ms. Valdez."

Anita agreed shakily, struggling to put her feelings in order as they joined the crowd drifting across the county fairgrounds. Jack Hayden was stirring up emotions she didn't know she had!

"I apologize for being improperly dressed, Anita," Jack said, studying the crowd as they walked along.

"What are you talking about now?" He was wearing jeans that fit too darned well and a knit shirt that practically obligated one to be impressed by the muscular chest filling it. Indecently attractive, yes, but improperly dressed? The man's mind seemed to operate...differently, to say the least.

"No hat, no boots," he explained, lifting one foot to show the expensive athletic shoes he wore.

When she reached up as though to slide her fingers through his thick, soft-looking hair, he grinned and said, "Forget the hat comment."

She pulled her hand back as if burned. What was she doing? This man confused her—made her forget her responsibilities, made her remember she was a woman. Her cheeks burned at how easily he could distract her from her duty, from reality, from everything but him. It was crazy!

"Say, where do people around here buy their clothes? Mail order catalogs?"

Well, that undistracted her! "We're just a little farther from the mall parking lots, that's all, Jack. You're not on Mars!"

A man sat behind a folding table at the tent's entrance. "That'll be eight-fifty."

Jack handed over some money and accepted two ticket stubs in return.

"You gonna have a decent season this year, Coach?"

"Oh, well, the kids are working hard." He nodded at the man, then put his hand under Anita's stiff elbow and guided her swiftly into the tent.

"Get used to it, Coach," Anita advised, her dark eyes flashing as they reached the long tables manned by people taking turns piling huge amounts of food onto plates. "Everyone in Larson is mad about football—except me."

Jack hesitated. Maybe after she ate, Anita would be in a more accommodating mood to discuss the subject calmly.

"I'm still getting to know the kids. I've got lesson plans to prepare. I don't know any of the teams we play. And you're mad *at* football."

"Yes, and you won't change my mind, if that's the idea."

Jack liked her straightforwardness, if not her declaration. He'd played games too long; it was refreshing not to. "I agree there are more important things to do with one's life." Jack tried to tell Anita with his eyes what some of those things were. "But you have to admit that organized sports offer opportunities for kids to enjoy themselves, to learn discipline and cooperation, to release pent-up energy."

"I don't have to admit anything," Anita said, but apparently didn't want to start a full-blown argument in front of the potato salad. "And I'd keep that attitude quiet, if I were you. Football's the state religion in Texas—and winning is everything."

"I signed a one-year contract, but if that's why they hired me, this may be the shortest job tenure in history."

Jack followed Anita to a table in the shade. He aimed dutiful smiles at the other people there, but kept his attention on his companion.

This woman makes me feel things I never thought I would. I don't want to argue with her, especially not on our first real date. Shouldn't I look out for my own interests? he wondered, then remembered Jesse's happiness and Danny's hopeful looks, their shy, impassioned pleas at practice and his promise to them.

"About your brother, Anita—"

Her dark eyes met his and held them until he dropped his gaze. "How do you like the brisket?" she asked firmly.

Jack obediently dug his fork into a slice of meat and transported a bite to his mouth.

"Brisket's great," he said after swallowing. "Tastes good between a rock and a hard place."

"What?"

"Nothing." Jack glumly prodded the meat again.

The afternoon passed in a haze of building heat, lifesaving breezes, friendly games of horseshoes and introductions to an endless stream of people.

"I've never met so many people in my life at one time," Jack said during a momentary lull.

"You used to put sixty thousand people in the seats every week."

"I didn't have to remember their names," Jack replied.

"You don't have to remember these."

"Oh, it's good PR," Jack said carelessly. "I'm beginning to feel deprived with only one sister, though. Is everyone in Larson related?" he asked before resuming his concentration with the next arrivals. "You're Dale's brother? And Danny's?"

The light was ebbing into true twilight now, though the air was still warm. The man nodded. "Ed Pawelek. Vern's our uncle. You better stick with him, 'Nita, till he gets us all straight."

A woman in her early twenties appeared at Ed's elbow to smile and flutter her eyelashes at Jack. She wore a white halter top and short-shorts that accented her lush figure the way neon accents Las Vegas. "Hi, I'm Rita Pawelek," she purred. "Ed's sister. If Anita ever gets too busy, Coach Hayden, I'd be more than glad to...show you around."

Sorry, honey— I've already been most of those places. I don't care to visit them again, Jack thought, smiling politely.

"Cool off, Rita," Ed advised with a wry grin. "'Nita's got dibs on him for now. Maybe you'll get a turn later." As she flounced away, Ed said, "Don't worry—she's harmless. Now, 'Nita—if he don't two-step to suit you, give me a holler."

Jack put his arm possessively around Anita's shoulder and flashed a primitive male smile he hadn't known he was capable of producing. "I don't two-step at all, Ed, but if it's important, I'll learn."

Ed grinned and tipped his hat, acknowledging the message. "Dance with who brung ya, I always say." He drifted off in a way Jack decided only large Texas cowboys could.

"Dancing's big around here, huh?" Jack asked before Anita could do more than remove his arm and part those enticing lips slightly.

She meant to tell Hayden she didn't appreciate his me-Tarzan, you-Jane act—or his attitude about Larson's idea of fun. The guy had a great body and personality, but these remarks about small-town life...

She knew why he was pursuing her—it was her own motive for prolonging the chase that really stumped her. *Why don't you just tell him to get lost?* she asked herself.

Because she couldn't. Couldn't resist the gorgeous man's look of hopeful anticipation. And she was selfish. Just for tonight, she wanted to forget her responsibilities and be a young woman with nothing more to worry about than flirting with a platinum member of the opposite sex.

Part of Anita questioned her right to use Jack. Subtle, scheming recruiter or not, he didn't deserve such treatment. He hadn't done anything to her. *Except kiss her like she'd never been kissed before!*

"I may have two left feet, but I'm willing to learn."

"Rita would be glad to teach you," she said finally.

Jack shook his head. "I want you, Anita."

The way he looked when he said it! He wasn't talking about dancing; desire burned deep in those clear hazel eyes. Her tingles were back in full force. She must be nuts, getting involved with a football coach. Hollywood Hayden, no less.

She wasn't in Jack's league, or even Rita's, but Anita had dated a fair amount, including that two-faced doctor—with lukewarm results. She'd certainly never reacted to anyone so quickly and so strongly before.

Until now, she'd thought those feelings and urges might only awaken after marriage. But Jack Hayden had been encouraging them since the instant they'd met.

Why not sample a few of the sensual delights Jack's kiss promised? Jack was the one who said they should separate the personal from the professional. And nurses were trained to do that.

Anita lifted her chin. "Okay, let's two-step. Come on."

She led him into the concrete-floored barn where the dance was getting underway. Jack acted game, but his rubber soles were a hindrance, sticking to the floor instead of sliding.

He managed a passable schottische and cotton-eyed joe; he even tried the chicken dance, laughing as he squawked and flapped his arms, but about halfway through, he mumbled an apology and practically galloped out of the dance hall.

Anita meant to let him go, but noticing Rita's interested gaze, followed Jack outside. She had to run to catch up. Finally, he slowed down, then stopped to lean against an obliging tree trunk.

"What kind of trees are these with the thin, feathery leaves?" Jack's question came out in an almost normal tone moments after she reached him.

"They're mesquites." Anita patted the rough bark affectionately, weak with relief she had no business feeling over any darned thing this man did or said. She should have let him go, she told herself, but self wasn't listening. Self was tingling again. And liking it.

Anita took a deep breath. *He just got bored with our unsophisticated entertainment.* And she didn't care what Hollywood Hayden did, thought, believed or imagined. *Or wanted.*

"Jack, I don't understand what happened in there."

"Nothing. I thought I'd made enough of a fool of myself for one night." Jack's clumsy attempt to gloss over his abrupt exit was somehow endearing.

Anita put her hand on Jack's arm in a sympathetic gesture that instantly became more. Without a word, his head bent, hers lifted, and their lips met in a mutual hunger that grew hungrier, more demanding as rapidly as it was satisfied. As his tongue explored the interior of her mouth, her hands tugged his shirt loose and slid underneath the cotton knit, her palms spreading velvet fire as they smoothed over the hard, muscular planes of his chest.

Flames raced through them as their kiss grew hotter and deeper.

"Anita." Jack ground out her name as he pressed against her, his body telling her how she affected him. "You're so... I've never felt anything like this before."

If he'd dumped a bucket of live bait on her, it couldn't have broken the spell any quicker. She jerked her hands from beneath his shirt, flattened her palms against the fabric and pushed him away.

She looked at him in the blades of light coming from the exhibit hall's doorway. He stood with his arms loose at his sides. The stupor act made her madder than ever. She stomped her foot. "You can come up with a better one than that, Jack Hayden. Anyone who kisses like you do has felt like this before. Plenty of times!"

"But I haven't," he protested.

"You've certainly had enough opportunities with your...groupies, haven't you?" Anita cried.

"Don't forget the starlets," Jack retorted, then inhaled and let it out slowly. "How many opportunities have *you* had, Anita?" The quiet question restored a semblance of control. Muted laughter and music drifted from the dance hall; the smell of night on the last summer grasses reached her nostrils, mixing with the scent and taste of Jack Hayden.

She took another deep breath and answered just as quietly, "Enough." *Enough to know I'm just a beginner.*

"Enough to know what you want?" he asked after a slight hesitation.

"I don't want anything, remember? You can kiss like the dickens, Jack Hayden, but I'm not interested in much beyond what we just had."

"Which was?" As if he urgently needed a definition! Had he been in a coma the whole time?

"A brief, mutually pleasurable interlude." She turned away and crossed her arms to make her pronouncement believable. And caught herself waiting breathlessly for his response.

"It was that," he agreed. "I'd like it to be the start of something more, but I've only got a year here—I don't know how slow I can go." He touched her shoulders lightly, then dropped his hands and said, "Look, Anita, maybe I'm not used to village life, and I'm definitely not good with words, but believe me, I'm not trying to seduce you into letting Jesse play football."

She spun around, and it wasn't the speed of the turn that made her dizzy. It was the sheer magnetism of the man facing her. Jack Hayden made her burn, made her tingle in ways nobody else ever had. *If I let him know how much he affects me, I'll be a sitting duck.* And darn it, her anxiety about Jack had nothing to do with Jesse. "Let's leave my brother out of this."

"Fine with me. Can you?"

She could hardly remember her name around this man, let alone answer difficult questions. So she said, "I think I'd like to go home now."

He fished a set of keys out of his jeans and tossed them to her. "Take the car. I can walk home from here. Thanks for the... interesting date, Anita. I enjoyed parts of it." Before she could say anything, he disappeared into the darkness.

She stared after him, then gave a soft snort at his nonsense. "As if he thinks I don't know what he's up to." But it wasn't his silly attempt at a grandstand exit that preoccupied her while she found her brother and made arrangements to return Jack's car.

No, what held Anita's attention like a snake's warning rattle was the still-throbbing imprint of his lips on hers, the memory of her hands cool on his warm skin, and most dangerous of all, the primitive, elemental yearning that still burned deep within her, ignited by his touch.

It threatened to drive every ounce of cold sense right out of her body and replace it with fire. *If you're smart, you'll avoid Jack Hayden like an IRS audit,* she told herself. But how?

For the first time in Anita's life, she thought Larson might be too small.

Chapter Four

"What's the point?"

"Keep your voice down, Jesse," Anita cautioned, miserable with frustration. Great way to end a day—arguing with a teenager. It was almost midnight and they were on the porch, but the windows were open, the family sleeping.

"Is this better?" he whispered sarcastically, then repeated his question, "What's the point of practicing if I'm never going to play? Do you want me to get down on my knees and beg?"

"Jesse! Try to see my side." She wanted his understanding, not just his obedience.

The boy slumped on the porch steps. The yard light illuminated his downturned mouth and rebellious chin, his clenched hands. "Why can't you see mine?" he asked, turning to look up at her.

"I do, Jesse." It was so hard for her to say no to the one thing he enjoyed, but somebody had to think of his safety and his future.

"What did Coach Hayden say?" Jesse demanded. "Did you listen to anything he said?"

Yes. She'd heard him counting the days until he could leave Larson. And worrying about replenishing his wardrobe. "About what?"

"About me playing! He said he'd talk to you. Said he might know enough adult buzzwords to convince you." Jesse kicked his foot at the step. "You didn't even listen, did you?" *You don't care.* The silent accusation cut the midnight air like a karate chop.

It was so unfair! Anita controlled her childish reaction, determined to stay in charge—of something! "He didn't say anything." *Not about football.*

"You probably didn't let him."

Anita blinked. Jesse was absolutely right. Jack had tried, she realized, but he'd given up pretty easily—to focus on seduction! And darned successfully, too. With a sense of having stepped in quicksand, Anita tried to defend herself without giving anything away.

"Look, Jesse, even if he was incredibly eloquent, the answer is still no. Kids are seriously injured every year playing contact sports. Do you want to jeopardize your future for a stupid game?" Before he could answer, she rushed on. "And you're old enough to accept the situation instead of chewing on it every five minutes like a dog with a bone!"

"But, 'Nita! Me and Danny waited three years to be the starters. It's not fair to leave the whole team stranded just 'cause you gotta show me who's boss."

Jesse's charges left Anita speechless. Her brother exhibited his fair share of adolescent exaggeration, but this... Something inside her registered the extent of his desperation. It almost matched her own.

"I'm not trying to show you who's boss, Jesse," she insisted. He'd touched a raw and very insecure nerve. "I'm trying my best to finish raising you. Believe me, I wish Mama and Papa were here to do it, but—"

Jesse jumped up. "You're not the only one who misses them, 'Nita," he said. "And you can't take their place. Nothing's the same!" He ran inside and Anita heard him closing the door to the room he shared with Petey.

She stared at the night and felt like crying. She understood Jesse's desire for a return to normal life. She wanted to do the same thing, but how could they do that? Things were different now.

Papa had been proud of Jesse's athletic ability. But he hadn't had Anita's precise knowledge of the dangers involved.

Anita buried her head in her hands, momentarily overwhelmed. For one second, she felt Jack's strong arms holding her, her cheek leaning against his hard chest, his hazel eyes gazing down at her telling her everything would be okay.

She stood up abruptly. Jack Hayden didn't want to comfort her or help her parent a teenage boy—a job she was totally unprepared for and probably messing up royally. Jack was only looking out for his own interests, except that today at the picnic, he hadn't really pursued the subject of Jesse's joining the team.

Anita sighed again in the warm dark night. How did single parents juggle all the emotional demands? *First, delete extraneous personal temptations with hot hazel eyes....* Ha! She'd have better luck getting Jesse to be reasonable.

"I sure hope I get the hang of this soon," she murmured to the darkness.

Crickets chirped encouragingly, but provided no guidance. Anita went inside and crept quietly into the room she shared with little Leticia, who slept like a log. Maybe she could find a small house to rent near the junior college. She punched her pillow. Jesse wasn't going to like that, either. He wanted to go away to school, but she just couldn't afford it.

Anita finally fell asleep under a heavy blanket of inadequacy.

* * *

Jack shrugged into his lucky navy blazer and adjusted the knot on his tie. Picking up his class folders with their rosters and lesson plans, he headed for the door of his apartment and his first day of school. And Anita. All day every day in the same building, they were bound to run into each other.

He hoped he still had some of his old charm left. Because Jack had reached a decision. Jesse's talent and desire to participate could be used to ease the boy's emotional difficulties. Regardless of the effect on Jack's personal interests, he had to convince Anita to let her brother play.

Given a chance, Jack thought he could help the boy. That was the most wonderful discovery he'd made in Larson—after finding Anita Valdez, of course. As a coach, he could make a difference. These kids were still impressionable. Young enough to learn and change and grow; old enough to understand and choose. If their legal guardians would cooperate!

Jack's first-day jitters disappeared. He gave his lucky blazer a pat—if it worked, he'd see her this morning. They'd *have* to talk to arrange something about picking up his car from her place. He started to set the dead bolt, then recalled his landlord's puzzled remark. "Hey, Jack, I came over to fix that leaky faucet th'other day—but you'd locked your door! Is something wrong?"

Jack was trainable. He flipped off the dead bolt, stepped through the front door and closed it behind him with a brief prayer for the safety of his stereo.

His car sat at the curb. Jack hurried down the sidewalk, then steadied himself with a hand on the hood as he stepped off the curb. Cold. The darned car had been there all night.

Leaning down, he peered through the tinted window. His concerns about his stereo eased—his keys were inside.

As he settled into the driver's seat, Jack pointed out to himself that Rita Pawelek was unmarried, possessed a great figure and an apparently willing disposition.

No use. Anita had the full, undivided attention of Jack Hayden's heart. He might be unable to change Anita's mind about Jesse, but he had to investigate her feelings for Jack Hayden.

Three minutes later, he walked into school, inhaling the ever-present smell of chalk dust and ballpoint ink. The halls were filled with boisterous groups of kids, some of whom called out greetings as he passed.

Checking room numbers in the high-school wing, Jack thanked heaven for everything that had led him to Larson and Anita. His knee injury was probably the best thing that had ever happened to him.

Jack freely admitted he'd been a jerk, but he wasn't stupid. During his six months of excruciating physical therapy, he'd learned more than how to make a reconstructed knee behave. He'd learned that ordinary people were the luckiest people on earth if they had a foundation of support to help them face the hardships life could throw at even the most fair-haired, harebrained football star.

Maybe he wasn't any good at being normal.

He'd tried. Gone back to school to finish his degree, then cycled through some pretty awful jobs and some pretty dull relationships. Including that woman in Ohio—Miranda—he'd gotten close that time. There'd been no spark, but she'd allowed a steady, if slightly sterile relationship. She'd even let him stay over a couple of times, and he'd decided it was the best he could hope for and prepared to make a permanent commitment. Then that TV feature dredged up his past and Miranda had shown him the door without delay. Funny, he couldn't recall her face, though he remembered worrying about her being his last chance.

He hadn't known there was an Anita Valdez somewhere, waiting for him.

Not exactly waiting, Jack. "Uninterested." When she kissed him like that? It was the worst nonsense he'd ever heard, including some of the gobbledygook he came out with. Jack patted his lucky blazer one more time. *Come on, coat, do your stuff!*

The first students strolled into class, giving him calculating once-overs. Did he look like a heavy homework-giver? Jack tried to put on a poker face, but couldn't manage it. He grinned at the kids; they grinned back.

Jack took roll, trying to match names to faces. As he assigned someone to pass out textbooks, Jack began to worry that his blazer's luck had run dry. He stepped out to put his attendance report in the holder beside the door.

And there she was, her arm around a nervous youngster. Jack gazed happily at his midnight-haired Anita.

The sparkle in her eyes as she met his gaze caused a stirring below his belt. Thank heaven for pleated trousers!

"Okay, thanks, Ms. Valdez." The girl hurried off.

"We need to talk, Anita." Jack glanced at his chattering class—they wouldn't miss him until Christmas.

"About what?" Her question was brusque, but the corners of her mouth twitched and her head moved, making her hair shimmer in the romantic, fluorescent light—Jack decided her tone was a smoke screen.

"About your brother." With his reply went a side order of slow, sexy smile that made her cheeks pink becomingly. "When would be convenient?"

Anita was immune to his smarmy come-on smile—except that her heart beat faster every time it appeared. "Never, Mr. Hayden. My mind's made up."

Jack's eyes grew wide enough for her to see the gold rings around the outer edge of the now-brown orbs. "But, Anita, you haven't even heard my argument!" he exclaimed.

"I don't need to!" Her full lower lip flattened its adorable curve into a straight line and her eyes became as hard and dark as coal. "This is my brother we're talking about, Jack," she added in a low, smoking voice. "The only family I have left. So forget it. Just forget it."

Beneath the surface of her eyes, Jack saw something hurting. He remembered lashing out during rehab to release his own pain and frustration.

"And forget *me,*" Anita added quietly and turned away.

Forget her? No way. Anita Valdez was under his skin—but she had something else underneath hers. A thorn named fear. And another called grief.

Jack played with the knot of his tie, steeling himself for the struggle he saw ahead. The struggle between what she feared and what Jesse needed. The struggle between the feelings she had about Jack Hayden the man, that he'd tasted in her fiery kiss, and the ones she held about Hayden the football coach.

"I can't, Anita." He kept his voice low, too, although she was moving away from him down the hall. "I can't forget your kiss, the way your hands felt on my skin...." When she turned, he looked deep into her eyes and smiled gently. "I don't think you can, either, but I promise I won't push you."

He put his hand on the classroom door frame for balance and said, "Maybe I'll see you in church." Then he winked at her.

The infuriating man's wink set off disturbing, long-lasting tremors inside Anita.

Luckily, the new school year kept her too busy to ponder Jack's statement more than a few hours every morning and a few more every afternoon—and practically all night every night. When she did get her mind off Jack, Jesse usually drooped into sight.

Every conversation they had eventually touched on his participation in that darned contact sport. She wanted Jesse happy, but did that mean she had to worry herself to death? She patiently explained the concept of risk management to him, but Jesse never heard a word of her logical, detailed thesis.

Instead, like the rest of the school, he hung on every word uttered by Hollywood Hayden.

Jack. The location of her office required Anita to pass his classroom frequently. Each time, he was absorbed in his class—leaning forward, listening intently, or talking animatedly and gesturing with a piece of chalk. *Acting like a devoted teacher. And looking attractive as hell.*

She avoided the school cafeteria, scheduled home visits for the times Jack might be looking for her to "talk," but she couldn't escape him completely.

Wednesday night, Anita passed the kitchen doorway; Jesse was at the table with Petey and an open English book. "I gotta keep my grades up in case Coach can persuade 'Nita to let me play," he informed his cousin.

Jesse had nearly failed last spring. That he was now studying without prompting was a victory Jack couldn't appreciate. But Anita could because she hated nagging as much as she hated arguing. Tears welled up at this tiny step forward. And yes, they were tears of gratitude.

"A football coach caring about grades?" she asked casually as she entered the room to get a cup of coffee.

"School rule is no pass, no play. Coach's personal rule is you've gotta have at least C's," Jesse responded. "Coach says you need a strong foundation, no matter what you do in life."

Petey's wide-eyed attention to Jesse's ringing conviction indicated another Hayden convert. Anita nodded to hide her chagrin. First, those bone-melting kisses and now lessons in motivating kids. The man was pure danger to a vulnerable woman.

When she saw him the next morning, a head above the sea of students surging through the halls, she knew she ought to thank him. He smiled his electric charming smile... and just before the crowd swallowed him up, he *winked.*

Ridiculous. Two hazel-eyed winks didn't have the power to make her heart leap and her insides twirl.

It was unlikely that Jack Hayden had any interest in forming an emotional attachment. All he'd mentioned was kissing, dancing and "getting acquainted." And Larson's rusticity. And that they only had a year.

Unfortunately, the reminder didn't loosen the still-tightening coils of desire generated by the memory of his mouth on hers. Those winks of his created longings that defeated their philosophical differences.

She needed a good dose of harsh reality to counter Jack Hayden's warm-fuzzy charisma. And she knew, after a phone call, where to find it.

The rehabilitation center at Gonzales was pleasant, well staffed and highly regarded. A cheerful physical therapy intern directed Anita to the proper room. After a second's hesitation, Anita tapped lightly on the half-closed door.

"What is it now?" a young voice asked tiredly.

Anita entered and smiled at the room's occupant, a large-boned boy with straight black hair and naturally bronzed skin. Seated in a wheelchair facing the window, he was wearing a T-shirt, warm-up pants and socks. Shoes were useless, he informed her with a scowl as he spun the wheelchair and caught her inspection.

"Marco Lopez?" Anita asked in her bright, professional nursing voice.

"What are you? Another torture expert?"

"I'm Anita Valdez."

The boy looked blank. She thought back—she'd been away from Larson almost half this kid's life.

"Maybe you know my brother Jesse."

"Jesse? Sure. So is this charity work or a pity tour?"

He had a right, no doubt, to his anger, but what good did it do him? She watched his fingers fiddle on the spokes of the wheel.

"Sorry, Ms. Valdez," he said after a few seconds. "I, uh, appreciate your visit. It's just—"

"Just what?" she prompted, her heart breaking for this poor kid.

"Nothing." He frowned deeply, then raised his hands, palms upward. "Look, I'm still adjusting to this." Another gesture encompassed his physical disability, the rehab center, the long, difficult future.

"The doc keeps saying I'm lucky I've got the use of my arms, so I oughta quit complaining.... But it's not fair!"

he burst out, his mouth returning to its apparently perpetual pout.

Anita looked helplessly at the youngster, who finally said, "So what's new in good old Larson, Ms. Valdez?"

Nothing, and that's what she liked about it. Nothing changed very fast.

"I was supposed to be back in school by now, but—" Marco broke off, ducking his head. "The doc says I'm not working as hard as I could, but what's the point?"

What's the point of self-pity, either? Anita thought.

Marco roused himself. "Sorry," he said awkwardly, then added with unfeigned interest. "Say, I hear we got a new coach this year. Hotshot from California."

Anita groaned. Had the injury to Marco's spinal cord affected his brain? She decided that men, regardless of age, were not part of the evolutionary chain, but a species totally alien to the solar system!

She didn't stay long after that. And all the way home, Marco's parting words echoed through her brain.

"I'd give anything to play for that guy. Wow. Hollywood Hayden."

Anita had been unable to stop a gesture at the boy's wheelchair and a strangled "Even that?"

"Well..." The kid hesitated, then nodded. "What a thrill to play for the best!"

She knew without any reflection that Jesse felt the same. She'd be the first to agree that kids needed role models and heroes, but a superjock wasn't— Then she remembered a few times during her own adolescence when logic had carried no weight.

Anita took out some of her frustration on the gas pedal, pushing the speed limit on the deserted road. "I think I'll run for president when I'm old enough," she told the steering wheel. After wrestling with parental decisions, being president would be a cakewalk!

As she turned off the highway at the Dairy Queen, a possible compromise occurred to her. She wouldn't mention it to anyone yet, though; it required further careful consideration.

Anita had told Jack that Texans take their football seriously, but he hadn't understood *how* seriously. He began to "get it" when the head cheerleader cornered him at noon Friday to discuss the agenda for the season's first pep rally in terms appropriate to the planning of a summit meeting.

"Pep rally, Marci?" Kind of a cute idea, he thought.

"Yes, Coach. Every Friday during football season, we have fifteen-minute early dismissal—"

"Why skip fifteen minutes of school for a pep rally?" Jack asked.

"So the buses can still get the farm kids home in time to do their chores," Marci explained. "Now, first we'll introduce the players and the Spirit Club officers, then the pep squad will perform, the band will play the school song and we'll have short speeches by the Booster Club president and the coach. That's you."

Jack smiled dutifully as Marci giggled at her own wit. He wondered who would be left to introduce everyone to.

He found out. At two forty-five that afternoon, the gymnasium filled to sardine capacity with students, teachers and apparently every parent and alumnus not incarcerated or hospitalized. As Jack waited his turn, inspiration attacked him.

All week, he'd been trying to corner Anita, but she'd eluded him, staying behind a barricade of moving kids. While the pep rallied, Jack put together an incredibly brilliant tactical plan that would deliver his objective right into his territory, where week after week he could wear down her defenses.

"Without further ado, I'd like to introduce our new head football coach—Mr. Jack Hayden!"

Marci, the perfect cheerleader: bouncy, peppy, never bothered by facts. Jack was the *only* football coach. He'd just discovered that Bubba's father was the Booster Club president; perhaps he could suggest a dad or two willing to help Jack run the practices. Organization wasn't his best skill, but he knew how to utilize available resources.

Stepping to the microphone, Jack looked over the sea of excited faces. His team, including Jesse Valdez because he'd practiced with them all week and Jack was a born optimist, was lined up at the front of the gym, wearing mesh jerseys over their shirts and jeans, appearing much smaller than they should to play a contact sport. Looking at them, Jack was gripped by sudden fear. Maybe Anita was right.

Come on, Hayden. Where's some of that smart-alecky cockiness you patented, now that you need it?

Jack cleared his throat and looked at the expectant crowd. He had no idea what to say to these people, but they were silent, apparently waiting for pearls of wisdom.

As he nervously thanked Marci for her kind introduction, he spotted Anita, hidden behind a row of pom-poms, a half smile lighting her face. His nerves faded. He knew what to say; he knew what he wanted. Anita.

And he had one crucial asset. Personal experience. His life, too, had changed drastically overnight. He understood some of what Anita felt about suddenly losing her parents and taking on responsibility for a youngster. Heck, wasn't that what he was doing this year, too?

But Anita and Jack weren't the only ones with problems. Jesse had his share, too. The boy needed the discipline and the physical exertion of participating in organized sports. Jack had sworn to corner Anita, even though he was probably sounding the death knell to his personal chances with her by championing Jesse's cause.

His first impression of Larson had been so erroneous. Too small—*ha!* The town was big enough to contain the woman who made him feel things, want things he'd never thought he could have. Jack was determined to explore the woman, the feelings, the wanting. He was also determined to get Jesse on the playing field.

Jack cleared his throat. He was going to try to have his cake and eat it, too. Unless he ended up eating crow for shooting off his mouth again.

He focused on Anita and his nerves disappeared. The words began to flow like honey. "Ladies and gentlemen, Larson students. As we begin a new season, I want to say that your team's been working very hard. We've had to start from scratch with a new coach and we're not sure he knows what he's doing—" he waited for the laughter to die down "—but I hope we'll give him a chance.

"Seriously, you-all—see, I'm learning to speak Texan." That got another laugh; behind the shivering pom-poms, Anita smiled and his heart started its bass-drum imitation. "The team's ready to take the field tomorrow and do their best. And, ladies and gentlemen, win, lose or draw, I'm proud of every one of these players."

There was a moment of silence. Jack held his breath. Had he said something wrong? He could accept disapproval for himself—heck, he should be used to it by now—but he didn't want any of it splashing onto these kids. As he searched for some way to undo whatever damage he'd done, the gym erupted in a frenzy of cheering. Jack observed it for a minute, then held up his hand for silence.

"I also want to thank some people for ensuring the Fighting Badgers have a successful season. First, Mrs. Sloan, sponsor of the spirit groups. Second, Elmer Wiatrek, who informed me he'll drive the bus so we arrive at the away games on time—" More applause and laughter. Jack used the time to quiet his resurging nerves. The strong-spirited, deeply resistant Anita Valdez might publicly call him a liar—or worse—without turning a hair. Did the heat of her kisses mean she felt enough for him not to? Jack took a deep breath; he was about to find out.

"And finally, I'd like to thank Nurse Valdez, who's agreed to stand by on the field in case of medical emergency." Like a silent movie, he watched her mouth open, saw her scowl, while the crowd's applause drowned her response. Jack hurried on, "I'm not promising we're going to be tough this year, but she'd better bring along plenty of bandages—for the other guys!"

Marci had a perfect sense of timing. As though they'd rehearsed it, she immediately signaled the band to play the fight song and led the cheerleaders in a riotous binge of jumping and cheering as the players exited the gym.

Jack ducked out with them. Yes, he was a coward, he sought to escape Anita's wrath under the protection of children. Whatever worked.

He got halfway across the parking lot. "Just a minute, Coach Hayden!"

He turned around slowly—and was mesmerized again by her breathtaking, fiery beauty. *She'd kill me if I told her she's beautiful when she's angry,* he thought. *That's progress. I'm learning to recognize what not to say—before I say it!* As she approached, Jack put on his heartiest smile and thought hopefully about all that passion, redirected. "Anita! How are you?"

She halted close enough to send her soft floral scent into his nostrils. They stared at each other for a lifetime of four or five seconds. "I'm fine," she said at last, the words slowly rasping out like sandpaper on rough wood. "A little overwhelmed by my own generosity."

A sheepish smile accompanied by a quick, light touch on her arm. "Anita, I can explain—"

"I'm sure you can." He thought a ghost of a smile flickered across her mouth, but he might have been mistaken. She crossed her arms and said, "I'm sure you can make your volunteering my services sound so innocent, so logical, I'll forget everything I know about you, about the dangers of contact sports, and—"

"Please." He cut off her speech with one finger against her lips. "If you could have seen Jesse in the locker room with the others—chattering away, excited as all get-out. I'm sure you know how important it is for kids his age to have a sense of belonging, but I respect your decision." Those hazel eyes were so inviting, begging her to trust him. "He asked me to talk to you, but I wasn't sure I should intervene. Then I thought maybe you were concerned about my lack of experience coaching boys this age, and—I can only describe it as inspiration. It came to me there at the mike. It's perfect! I'll feel better about letting the boys play full-out knowing you're right there in case anything happens. And it gives you a chance to observe the situation first-hand."

Anita stared at him at least two eternities, giving him a chance to lose himself in her deep dark eyes. He still couldn't decide—were they black or brown?

"I'll be hornswoggled," she said finally. "I knew you were going to do it. I told you I knew you were going to do it—and darned if you still didn't do it!" Her amazement was plain as plastic wrap.

"I'm not sure what you're talking about," Jack said cautiously, "but did I convince you to stand by as medical support?"

Anita nodded once, then turned and wandered away, muttering to herself. "How does he do that?" was the only phrase Jack understood.

He was too weak-kneed with relief to go after her. She hadn't killed him. He'd see her at the game. And he hadn't let Jesse down completely. He'd talked to her and she hadn't said no. She just hadn't said yes, either. Not yet.

Saturday night, the stadium lights blazed. The boys were nervous and excited; the crowd was eager and excited; Anita, herself, felt a little anxious as she stood behind the narrow wooden bench on the side of the field. The bands had played the national anthem and the school songs. The senior class chaplain had muttered a quick prayer over the squealing PA system. The new football season was about to start.

Jack had his hand on Jesse's shoulder and they were both looking hopefully in her direction.

Jack Hayden couldn't promise her that nothing would happen to Jesse on that darned football field. But that was about all he couldn't do to her. The way he affected her insides with those expressive eyes, those little-boy grins—and those masterful kisses! He seemed so kind, so open, so concerned. He'd held Dale's newborn son with genuine awe and wonder—nobody could fake that, could they? That initial response to Jack Hayden the man was turning into a sensual longing that went off the scale.

And Jesse—she remembered how it felt to be seventeen. She knew how much it meant to him to be one of the Badgers. *As much as being part of Larson means to me.*

A stray thought zinged into her consciousness. Was she hiding behind Jesse? Wrangling with him over football to protect herself from risking a personal relationship with a man she didn't really know?

For the zillionth time, Anita wished Jesse wanted to compete in chess or table tennis. And why couldn't Jack be a nice feed-store owner or English teacher?

"Sis—" Jesse was banging his helmet against his knee while his eyes pleaded with her.

"One play," Anita said, naming the compromise she'd devised. "One play a quarter, but that's it."

She had to fight back tears when Jesse's grin appeared like a blinding spotlight and he grabbed her and hugged her.

"Thanks, Sis. Thanks!" He turned and raced over to Danny, who was fastening his chin strap. "Danny! Guess what?" The boys pounded each other in their excitement.

"Thanks, Anita. I appreciate the struggle you've gone through. I really think it's the best decision for Jesse." Jack's solid warmth was like a shield around her, but could it carry all the way out on the field to protect Jesse?

"And the team?" She was losing herself in his eyes again, right there in the middle of bedlam. She was spiraling into desire and heat and longing and she knew he was going with her.

"Team who?" he asked bemusedly, then an official's whistle broke the spell and Jack reluctantly went to work.

Anita edged closer as Jack gave the huddle of boys their last instructions. Maybe the way he treated the boys during actual competition would be a clue to the larger issue of his character, she thought. The last coach had harangued them, fired them up until they roared like mindless, angry bears.

"I'm proud of you guys," Jack was saying in a calm, everyday voice. "As far as I'm concerned, you're winners already—so just go out and do what we've done in practice all week, watch the ball, watch one another, be good sports. Have fun."

With a shouted, "Team!" the starters ran onto the field.

Anita's professional services were never required; all she did was watch Jack Hayden. Despite her very best intention to remain unmoved, his behavior fascinated Anita. She couldn't tell who was winning by watching Jack. Each time players came off the field, he had a word of praise for them. Each time he sent a boy out to play, Jack supplied him with encouragement to take along. Even the mistakes made by inexperienced and nervous young men received only calm, confident assurances they'd do better the next time.

Okay, his handling of the youngsters was impressive. So was his broad-shouldered form striding from one end of the bench to the other—even with that ever-so-slight limp. It was like watching a stallion strut, with a pebble in its shoe.

Before she knew it, the game was over and the Larson Fighting Badgers had won. After the midfield goodwill handshakes, Jack waded through cheering Badgers, offering individual praise, skillfully working his way steadily, purposefully toward her. Just as she thought about slipping away, her brother ran up and bear-hugged her. "Wasn't that a great game, Sis? Did you see me? Did you see how Danny threw the ball? And the way we forced turnovers? We never played like that before! Isn't Coach great?"

Well, she didn't think he was *great,* exactly, but his handling of the team did earn him some points. *For what? What happens if he scores enough points? Does he win Jesse full-time? Me as a love slave?* she asked herself while Jack drew nearer and nearer and her silly heart beat faster and faster. If he tried, would she let Jack kiss her again just because nobody made her tingle the way he did? Would he try?

"Come on, Jesse," she said urgently. "Let's go."

Jack was suddenly beside them, grinning down at her. "Hit the showers, son. I'll keep your sister company."

The way Jack handled the straggling well-wishers while they waited reminded her of his vast experience at being the center of attention. Yet, he modestly refused to take credit for the victory. He insisted the boys had won, not the coach.

"You ought to be a politician," Anita commented wryly as the last clumps of spectators drifted off.

"I'm going to be a basket case before the season's over," Jack replied, cupping her elbow with his palm. "Are the games always this packed or was it crowded because this was the first game?"

Anita looked up at him, trying unsuccessfully to ignore the tingles spreading from his touch. "Jack, last year the Badgers lost eight of ten games. This was not a particularly large crowd."

Jack's disbelief was plain. "Anita, those stands were almost full! There were more people up there tonight than I've seen the whole time I've been here—picnics included!'

"Jack, Larson's a rural community. The farmers and ranchers farm and ranch. They don't come to town every day to be counted, but they're going to watch their boys play, come hell or high water."

"Well, I wish you'd warned me. I thought I was going to die of fright when I saw that crowd."

Anita could only stare as his ridiculous statement spawned another torrent of distrust and doubt. Was he mocking her concern for Jesse or was he ridiculing Larson itself? The man was a record-setting, famous quarterback used to performing in front of trillions. How could he be nervous about a little high-school football game in Smalltown, Texas?

"I know it's silly, maybe," he confessed, as though reading her mind. His brandy-warm voice was almost as intoxicating as his touch. In its heat, as always, her doubts and fears seemed to fade like fog in sunlight. "But I'm pretty green as a coach. I didn't want the boys to feel bad if something went wrong."

He looked at her significantly.

She conceded. "Well, nothing went wrong tonight. You won."

"The boys won," he corrected her gently, curling his hand around her waist as they neared the gym's back door and were momentarily alone. "And nobody got hurt, so maybe you'll reconsider Jesse's participation limits. Let me buy you dinner. Dessert. Coffee. Uh, what do you say?"

Standing there in the shadows with his arms around her and his faint musky cologne in her nostrils, Anita was sorely tempted to make what could only be a huge mistake. Any woman would be flattered by Jack Hayden's attention, but Anita knew he had an ulterior motive—heck, the idiot had just admitted as much—and she'd already compromised as much as she could. *But wouldn't it be nice to know how he did that electric-tingle trick,* she mused, *so she could develop a method of neutralizing its effect?*

Jack's heady sensual appeal was hard to withstand, but Anita reminded herself firmly that Jack had a one-year contract, a Hollywood history and not an ounce of Hispanic blood. Not that it mattered to her, but... She suddenly knew that Jesse wasn't the only Valdez with something precious to lose in the Larson High athletics program. "Thanks, Jack, but—"

"Hey, Coach!" A gaggle of ebullient teenagers, Jesse in the middle smiling broadly, barged between the two adults. "We're all going to the Pizza Palace in Kenedy to celebrate—you gotta come!"

The players, damp-haired and overcologned, were physically separating Jack from the woman with whom he wanted to spend the rest of his evening. *For starters.*

Before he could protest, his eyes met Anita's.

He could hardly hide his glee at the look that passed between them. A shared look. A common thought. *A bond.* None of the boys would *dare* drink and drive with the coach around.

He'd take the brownie points. He needed them.

"Will you join us?" He gazed beseechingly at Anita as the boys clutched his arms and applied pressure.

Anita laughed and shook her head.

He waved farewell, silently vowing to spend time with Anita Valdez somehow, someplace. And if the subject of increasing Jesse's playing time never came up, Jack wasn't sure how heartbroken he'd be. He didn't want to argue with Anita, he wanted to charm her. Romance her. Court her.

Anita winked at him as the boys dragged him away.

That reminded him of his original clever plan. And the problem he'd discovered with implementing it. Larson didn't have a grocery store, but it had six churches. The solution slouched across Jack's field of vision. "Come on, Jesse, you can ride shotgun with me."

Chapter Five

When Anita walked into the church nursery the next morning, Jack was carefully accepting an infant and a diaper bag from a giggling mother. It was outrageous: he looked simply adorable as he awkwardly juggled the two items toward a crib and a cubbyhole. Anita smoothed down her pink cotton print dress, wishing it were silk, and waited to see if he figured out which went where.

"What are you doing here?" she whispered a moment later as she passed him to take Rose, the Muñoz's youngest, from her mother.

"I told you I'd see you in church, remember? Jesse said you work here in the nursery during the service, so..."

That darned sheepish grin is plain irresistible, Anita thought as she gave up and let it melt her heart again. Just this once.

Jack yawned. "Sorry. Those boys kept me out till two a.m.—I'm too old for such nonsense."

Anita started changing a diaper, smothering a protest that would reveal her growing vulnerability. This morning, Jack had covered his wide shoulders with a pale blue oxford-cloth shirt decorated with a tie; his long, muscular legs were hidden by superbly cut charcoal slacks. Jack Hayden was too virile, too masculine, too damned sexy to be too old for anything! What kind of bull was he slinging?

She knew what time they'd finished celebrating last night—she'd still been awake, reliving the sheer delight of his kisses, when the rumble of his sports car alerted her that he was depositing Jesse at home, safe and sound.

Anita studied the object of her late-night daydreams from beneath her lashes. Jack was leaning over the next crib, apparently absorbed in softly crooning to Joel Adams, who waved his tiny feet in the air. Maybe her heart needed proof that it was toying with disaster. *In the meantime,* that vulnerable part coaxed, *you could enjoy those sensual pleasures he advertises so nonchalantly—and so blatantly.*

"Boy, you're good at that." His praise was admiration, plain and simple. What kind of nut got excited over changing a diaper?

"I should be—I've probably done it a trillion times," she said.

"Wow. You're lucky."

The man was either certifiable or Hollywood wasn't what it used to be.

"Could you show me? I told the Sunday school director I knew how, but..." That charming boyish smile made another appearance with the same old effect: all sins forgiven. His warm personality and earnest charm always demolished her defenses the way chocolate ruins diets.

If she knew exactly who Jack really wanted with his persistent pursuit—*her or Jesse?*—maybe she could give him the cold shoulder without having it immediately melted again by his hot sweet voice or his warm hazel eyes. Then she could effortlessly resist him and get on with destroying Jesse's first happiness in months.... *Wait.*

Life had certainly gotten complicated since Jack Hayden moved from Hollywood to Larson, Texas! The only way to simplify it again was to refuse to have anything to do with him.

So when Jack asked her to dinner—with his cute smile and a baby draped over one massive shoulder, she accepted without a second's hesitation. Maybe *she* was certifiable!

"Thanks, Anita! I'll pick you up at six, okay?" His blazing smile negated the church's air-conditioning.

"Okay," she said weakly and tried to ignore the heat he created so easily. The pit of her stomach warned her she'd just made a terrible mistake. Her pulse, racing past, disagreed. Foolish pulse—remembering the way his kisses burned—sang, *We're alive.*

But Anita also knew that life sometimes hurt.

"So, are we stuck with Dairy Queen?" Jack asked as he helped Anita into the car. He'd already complimented her on her dress, a soft, clingy navy number that did delightful things to her figure and awesome things to his body.

The sun was low in the west, but the light would linger two more hours. He figured it would take at least that long to feed and cajole her into forgiving him for...well, for whatever. When the sun went down, he planned to kiss the living daylights out of her. That always seemed to vanquish her objections to him, momentarily at least.

"Something wrong with it?" Anita asked, one eyebrow lifted in unspoken challenge. Anita's arm's-length routine only served to harden his resolve—and that's not all. Luckily Jack knew how to pursue a goal with patient persistence.

So he produced a just-friendly smile and said, "I was hoping you knew someplace with a little finer ambience. If we were practically anyplace else in America, I wouldn't have to ask, but...the Pizza Palace in Kenedy isn't exactly my idea of intimate dining, either. So what do you suggest?" Out of the corner of his eye, he saw Petey and the littlest Valdez, Leticia, emerge from the house to lounge on the porch in an elaborately casual manner.

Anita looked at him. *She had some suggestions, all right.* Highly improper ones, prompted by the way Jack filled his starched white dress shirt and navy pleated slacks. And the way his hair brushed back from his temples, while one little strand fell deliciously over his forehead. Heck, even his bent nose was attractive. "How many times did you break it?" she said, to forget those improper suggestions and remember who he was.

"What?"

"Your nose."

"Er, twice. Never while dining, though."

Her laugh was sweet and clear and honest. Jack started the car abruptly, before his hands wrapped themselves around her shoulders and pulled her into an embrace so powerful it would blow her little cousins clear off the porch.

"The closest French restaurant's in San Antonio, but there's a place near La Vernia that has good steaks," Anita said as he headed down the driveway.

"Great. I have enough trouble with English."

"What about my language?"

His eyes left the road and locked on her mouth. "I intend to become fluent in it, through intense study."

"Spanish. I meant Spanish," Anita said faintly, blushing.

"That too, *señorita,*" he said with a grin.

The steaks were more than good, charbroiled to perfection, accompanied by crisp salad greens, fluffy baked potatoes and hot homemade rolls.

Jack kept the mood light during dinner by focusing the conversation on their childhoods. He learned that Anita's dolls wore splints and bandages regularly; he told her about his dad's getting in trouble for flying over the house on Jack's eighth birthday.

Over coffee and chocolate pie, he tried to casually introduce a more serious subject, but as usual, his attempt at subtlety was pretty clumsy.

"How long ago did your parents die?"

Anita's coffee cup clinked against its saucer. Jack's head was bent over his pie. The candlelight put amber highlights in his thick brown hair, making it seem warm and toasty, like everything else about him. Except this cold question.

She gave him a cold answer. "Nine months ago. In January."

His hand engulfed hers and squeezed gently. "Gosh, Anita, I'm sorry. It must have been a terrible shock."

Shock? What a small word to describe the array of emotions that had struck her when the police tracked her down in San Antonio to notify her. What a short word to describe the painful, life-changing aftermath.

But you did what you had to do. Though she had no idea how to raise a teenage boy, she was giving it her best shot.

Anita looked at Jack's puppy-dog eyes and almost believed he understood the pain and worry and doubt she struggled with daily. Almost. She looked down at his big, callused fingers covering hers. At the hands that threw touchdown passes in the Super Bowl and held starlets and models *and* French menus. Hollywood Hayden.

"How would you know?"

"My mother died of cancer while I was in college," he said softly. "I rushed through finals, but—I didn't get home in time."

Maybe he did understand a little about grief and sorrow.

"That was one reason I turned pro early. Football—"

"Football!" When nearby heads turned, Anita lowered her voice. "You're going to tell me sports helped you cope?" Clearly, she thought his idea of bereavement was pretty shallow.

Those warm hazel eyes heated like dry pinecones. "In a way, yes." Fork, pie, coffee, surroundings—all were forgotten as Jack leaned across the table, drawing her into his intense and powerful gaze. "Men are different, Anita. We don't talk about our feelings as easily as women do. The deeper and more important the emotion, the less we can put it into words.

"Men are doers. Action is our refuge. So, yes, football helped. It kept me busy and disciplined and motivated enough to get out of bed every day. It got me through the first dreadful months, until enough time passed that I could begin to feel my sorrow without being overwhelmed by it. I concentrated on each practice, each game, getting through the days one at a time until I could miss my mother without wanting to die, too."

The bleak look in his eyes was so exactly like the one she saw in Jesse's! Anita blinked back her own tears—did they think she didn't want Jesse happy again? She just wanted him safe, as well.

And she grieved, too—without blubbering to every person she met. "I–It's hard for me some days, too."

"I know it is," he said and his voice was sincere. Darn it, he *did* understand! "I'm just saying that Jesse would benefit from football as I did."

"I let him practice. And last night, he played four times. What more do you want?"

The waiter slid the bill onto the table and Jack slipped his credit card on top of it with practiced ease.

"I want Jesse to use what he's learning—so it doesn't seem as pointless as the rest of his life probably does right now. But I can't allow him to play another game like he did." He shook his head. "What you let him do yesterday night—it isn't safe."

"I let him? Isn't safe?" Her outrage practically melted the meringue on what was left of Jack's pie.

"He went on the field four times, Danny threw the ball to him four times. Next week's opponent will know how to defend that play—tackle Jesse. It's too dangerous."

"Jack—"

"I know you're concerned about his physical safety, Anita, but his mental health is also important. I'm not a psychologist, but I am a man. He'd benefit tremendously from being part of the team."

Anita studied him in the soft candlelight, while he added in a tip and signed the credit slip. Gosh, yes, Jack Hayden was a man. He of all people should understand male behavior.

Jesse spent countless hours with his friends, especially Danny Pawelek, but when she asked what they did, he mumbled, "Nothing."

When he came home from doing "nothing," though, Jesse was almost his old self for a while.

An image of Marco Lopez rose in her mind. If anything like that happened to her brother... But Jack was right—Jesse stood more chance of being injured if he only played a few times each game.

The quicksand was getting thicker, sucking her deeper.

"Well...that equipment they wear—how well does it protect them?"

Anita's lifted shoulders told him she was wavering. *Be persuasive, Jack.* "With the special neck pads and the new helmets, it's probably more dangerous to cross the main street in little old Larson at two a.m. on a Tuesday than to play high-school football, especially at this level."

"Little old Larson?"

Jack could have slapped himself.

Well, now that he'd stuck his foot in his mouth again, he might as well chew off the toes. "In this case, being so small is good. Larson's in the lowest division of Texas high-school sports. The Badgers and our opponents aren't those steroid-bulked monsters you see crunching one another on TV." Jack bit his lip. Crunch? Couldn't he use a more descriptive verb?

"They can still get hurt."

"Jesse already hurts, Anita." Jack knew she didn't care that Jesse's talent was a God-given gift the boy had a duty to develop; he knew she didn't care that when her brother was on the field, the whole team's caliber rose a notch. She just cared about protecting the only family she had left. And he could understand that, but...

"What if he plays half the game?" Jack suggested. "Anytime you think it's too dangerous, bench him. I'll back you up."

"Well..."

He could tell by the quirk of her luscious lips that she was vacillating. Jack escorted Anita from the restaurant and handed her carefully into his sports car. "Do you want to tell him or shall I?"

"I haven't said yes, yet, Jack," she said with a smile that sent his hope soaring.

"You will."

When he'd eased into the small car, folded his legs inside, snapped on his seat belt and started the engine, Anita said, "I'll think about it, but the experiment's off the minute his grades drop."

"That's another benefit of organized sports—they force the kids to be organized. Schedule their homework and so forth."

"You are a heck of a salesman, Hollywood."

"Only when the product's worth it—and the name's Jack. Plain Jack. Hollywood's in California."

Anita snorted softly. "I'll bet you miss it. You must be climbing the walls of *little old* Larson already."

Jack looked at the narrow strip of road illuminated by his headlights as they sped from one tiny dot on the map to another. He didn't bother to correct her. She'd see. "Oh, I've got big plans—they keep me busy," he said cheerfully and changed the subject. "Where's Jesse going to college?"

"The closest community college."

Her defensiveness was minimal. Like low-grade nuclear waste: only harmful over a long period of time. So Jack plowed on. "Jesse says he wants to go away to school. It's a good experience—"

"It's out of the question, too. Why don't you mind your own business, Jack?"

Anita bit her lip. Why did she react so strongly to Jack Hayden? One minute, she fantasized about his kisses, the next, she was snapping because he'd reminded her he didn't belong to Larson the way she did. *And they say teenagers had mood swings!*

Jack mumbled an apology and drove silently.

Anita pondered her confusion a few minutes, then her mind drifted back to its favorite subject: Jack Hayden.

"I guess you made a lot of money playing football."

Jack chuckled. "I wish. I was drafted just about last. Signed a minimum-salary contract. Before the big bucks could roll in, I was out of football. Back in school, finishing my degree so I could get a job like everybody else."

Anita looked at his profile. The dim lights of the dash etched his chiseled features with character and strength and sensitivity. The faint whiff of his understated cologne mingled with the cool night air and his own particular scent. He chuckled again and Anita felt his warmth and kindness reach out to her like a caress.

She smiled at his foolishness. The poor man was hopelessly misled. Jack Hayden was *not* everybody else!

He switched the conversation to general topics before she could ask any more questions. The sports car ate up the distance as they discovered they both liked old monster movies and disliked most rap music. The last few miles, Anita entertained Jack with outrageous-but-true tales of Texas politics.

She interrupted her graveyard-voters story. "Why are you slowing down? The speed limit's still fifty-five along here."

"I know," he admitted. "But we're only a few miles from your uncle's place."

"So?"

He tried, but he couldn't hear one decibel of disappointment in her question—she obviously didn't see things the way he did. Didn't feel about him the way he felt about her. Jack sighed as a flood of discouragement washed over him. He let the car accelerate slightly while he lectured himself back to an even keel. What did he expect—instant infatuation? Anita Valdez was a passionate woman who just wasn't thrilled by Hollywood Hayden. After the Miranda episode, he shouldn't be surprised.

Anita wasn't going to fall into Jack Hayden's arms after one steak dinner; he was an idiot to expect it. *I don't expect it,* he told himself. *I just want it! I want her!* "Well, er, I'm sorry to see the evening end so soon."

"We'll see each other tomorrow, Jack. Can't you live without me for eight hours?" There was mellow, sunny laughter edging her reply, laughter that revived his hope, fed his desire.

He gave a dramatic sigh to hide the depth of that desire. *No, I can't. I want to hold you close the next eight hours.* "It's not quite the same. We never get to talk at school. You're always surrounded by students."

"So are you. You shouldn't be so attractive, Jack. So exotic. The girls hang around you and the boys hang around the girls."

"Me? Exotic?" *She said I'm attractive! Holy cow, maybe my luck's changing!* He struggled against the urge to cheer like a lottery winner.

"Sure, you're the glamour boy from out of town. Heck, you're all the way from another state. That makes you practically a foreigner."

"I'll apply for Texas citizenship," he said absentmindedly. "What about dinner tomorrow? Without our fan clubs." The little red car crept through Larson's only stoplight, a single lamp flashing yellow, as he waited for her answer.

Then he remembered. "Wait—I'm busy tomorrow night."

Please let her silence be jealousy.

"Anita!" He pretended shock. "Your own hometown, too. The Booster Club meets Monday evenings. The coach attends every meeting." Jack tried to sound genuinely enthusiastic. "They even feed me supper. I'll share it with you," he added, hoping to entice Anita to attend so he'd have the pleasure of looking at her while the meeting dragged on.

"Well, you're certainly slipping right into Larson's lifestyle. Do you know what the Booster Club does?"

"I'm looking forward to finding out," he said, wondering what her tone was trying to convey. He also wanted to distract her from the fact that the car had drifted to a stop in front of the darkened house. Only one weak light burned atop a tall pole in the yard. Anita's uncle farmed their small acreage and her aunt ran the elementary-school cafeteria. *Thank you, early risers.*

Against his will—sort of—his attention fastened itself on Anita's mouth, barely hearing the words issuing from those lips made for his. Despite her disbelief, Jack never had kissed a woman the way he'd kissed Anita. He'd never felt for anyone what he felt for Anita: something so far beyond friendship, it was quite possibly a four-letter word. The recognition should have scared or astonished him. Instead, it thrilled him so much, he barely understood her next sentence.

"The Booster Club's a group of people who support the Badgers's athletic programs—"

"Ah, athletic supporters..."

"Jack, aren't you too young for that old joke?"

He ignored her criticism and his physical frustration; he was probably going to experience a lot more of both before he wore her down. "Monday-morning quarterbacks, huh?"

"They do some second-guessing," she admitted.

Jack remembered his volunteer coach plan. "Who's in the Booster Club?" he asked as his arm stretched slowly across the seat backs.

"Practically everyone in town."

The windows of the car were down; he could smell dew and earth and night beneath Anita's spring flowers. "Figures—what else is there to do in Larson on Monday night? Sounds like they might notice if I'm not there."

"You have such a flair for understatement, Coach Hayden."

As if someone had switched on a bad movie, he heard himself say, "And you have a flair for hot, deep kisses, Anita." Then his lips descended on hers and the already-familiar passion flared instantly, smothering his dumb line in smoke and heat. Their bodies leaned together across the space between the seats; she moved against him as their mouths shifted. More heat, more passion. His tongue stroked the interior of her moist, warm mouth; one of his hands moved up the front of her dress.

God! He dragged his control back from outer space and lifted his mouth slowly from hers. "I–I'm sorry, Anita. I can't seem to maintain any sort of decorum around you."

He waited for her to put him in his place, tell him she didn't want to kiss him, didn't want to see him, ever again.

Anita clicked open the passenger door and swung her feet out of the car. "You wreak havoc with my decorum, too, Jack Hayden." Her voice was strangely muted, as though buried beneath layers of the velvet night.

Then she was gone. Jack watched her small figure, barely visible in the faint light, climb the porch steps. She pulled open the screen door quietly and disappeared through the black rectangle of the doorway. For a moment, he was worried about her sleeping, defenseless, in that wide-open house, then he shook his head with a smile and started the engine, careful not to gun it.

Jack turned the car on the grass and eased it back to the road. *The whole county leaves their doors unlocked,* he reminded himself. *Because they feel safe.* He headed through the deserted streets of town to his own unlocked and no doubt undisturbed apartment. *What a hell of a place to raise kids. My kids.* Jack's smile was broad because he had a darned good idea who he wanted their mother to be.

And why. Jack pulled the car into the parking area behind his apartment, gravel crunching beneath the tires. Not because he was lonely or yearned for normalcy or wanted to Be Married or Play Daddy. But because he'd met her. *Her.* The woman he'd been looking for all his life. Suddenly, he saw that even his crazy Cinderella year with its flamboyant, headline-grabbing party mania had been a search for the right person in the wrong places.

What a fool! *She* was in Larson, Texas, all the time.

No, not all the time, he reminded himself. She'd left Larson and gone to San Antonio, only coming back to mother a teenager and work through her own grief.

Now came the monumental task of convincing her that they were made for each other. If Jack was pretty sure of one thing about Anita, it was that her emotional resistance to him ran DNA-deep. Months of work lay ahead, battling her prejudice against his occupation, his past, his broken nose—and whatever else stood in their way.

Jack pushed open his apartment door and went in, massaging the stiffness out of his knee. He could do it. He had to—the way Anita made him feel, the things he wanted with her... He wouldn't give up without a fight. Even if the waiting drove him crazy!

Jack showed up at the Booster Club meeting the next evening looking for Anita. Not for any kissing, either. Darn the woman! Before he could find her in the mass of people crowding the school cafeteria, he was caught and served a delicious dinner by a woman who spoke only Polish. Once the meeting was called to order, he gave up on his search for the moment. He listened to some tips on defeating the team's next opponent and made his volunteer-coach request. A platoon of helpers responded, and finally, during the business portion, he spotted his quarry.

After the meeting, with what he thought was a great deal of finesse, Jack intercepted Anita in the slowly exiting crowd and began edging her toward the door.

"Ya cut her out of the herd right slick, son. Had me a horse one time was almost that good," commented a smiling man with a weather-beaten face and scarred boots.

"Excuse me?"

After settling his straw cowboy hat on his head, the man chuckled and jabbed his thumb in Anita's direction.

Jack smiled grimly. "Can I buy you a soda, Anita?"

Anita's nod drew a rush of pleasure that almost drowned the anger he'd carried around all afternoon. Jack sighed inwardly. Anita the woman did things to his insides—delicious things. Anita the new parent did positively infuriating things to his head, but he couldn't stay mad at her; he knew she was doing what she thought was best.

Even when it wasn't.

They pulled into the Dairy Queen and Jack gave their order to a girl who was in his math class. "Two of those blizzard things. Surprise us with the flavors."

"Right away, Coach."

"Thanks, Trish," Jack said, then turned to Anita. "It's amazing.... I've only been here two weeks, but I bet I could go anywhere in town and know at least one person."

"Why sure. Everyone in *little old* Larson knows everyone else." There was a challenging note in her statement he didn't understand.

"Does that bother you?" Jack asked cautiously.

"No, but I grew up this way—it's probably intrusive to someone used to the anonymity of big cities. Of course, you weren't exactly anonymous. I'm sure you miss all the amenities, too...." Her voice trailed off, but Jack could see in the neon glare a rare look of wistfulness that twisted his gut, distracting him from his purpose. Affecting him so strongly was a talent Anita seemed to have in spades!

Did she miss San Antonio? Should he make up some plans to move there? Or be honest and tell her how much he was beginning to enjoy Larson's slower pace. Jack opted for neutrality, sort of.

"Well, I'm sure I can take it for a year. Actually, Larson has a certain charm. Great barbecue. Friendly people." Now he'd make a smooth transition. "Speaking of people—"

"Marco—" Anita said the name at the same moment.

She looked so troubled, Jack wanted to reach across and pull her into his arms, but Larson might never recover. The Dairy Queen was the local equivalent of CNN.

"Is he the reason?" His frustration made the question grate out. Anita didn't answer as Trish brought the frosty drinks.

Jack handed over one of the tall cups and waited until the carhop went back inside. "What happened, Anita? I mentioned playing the first half to Jesse and he looked so..." She must know how he looked: sullen, angry, desperate.

"It wasn't Marco, exactly. It was..." Her voice faded and Jack put his hand on her shoulder.

"What?" he asked softly. Jack was hurt that she didn't trust him, didn't think he was concerned for her brother's safety—but the curves fate had thrown her might scare anyone.

"I don't want to talk about it," Anita said shortly. Marco's mother had called to thank her for visiting the boy.

She kept seeing him in his wheelchair. How could she allow Jesse to take that risk?

Anita sighed. Sitting this close to Jack Hayden did terrible things to her resolve. He overloaded her senses until she could barely remember her own name.

"Well, I don't want to discuss it, either," Jack said, thinking of his own precarious position with Anita, "but I can't stand to see Jesse hurt—"

"Wait right there!" In a cloud of anger, Anita waved her drink at him. What insanity made her heart leap at a full view of his strong features, his chiseled mouth? "What the heck are you talking about?" she demanded.

"Changing your mind about letting Jesse play. I thought we'd decided."

She wasn't about to admit that she couldn't think straight around Jack or that maybe she'd overreacted to Mrs. Lopez's phone call. If parents weren't allowed to be confused occasionally, she was in trouble.

Anita twisted in the narrow seat of the car and poked a frantic finger at Jack. "*We* decided? Look here—he's *my* brother! *My* responsibility. I'm doing what I think is best for him."

"You're confusing him. It's more important to be consistent with kids than right."

"How dare you!" *How dare you be right?* Anita fumbled for the door handle, opened the car and started to get out. Unfortunately, she'd forgotten her seat belt was still fastened and she was unceremoniously jerked back in the seat.

Before she could try again, Jack's fingers circled her wrist. "Anita, look—there's a good example of risk and reward. You drive because you need to go places, even though it's not one hundred percent safe."

"Jesse doesn't need to play a dangerous game."

"But it's not just a game. Not for Jesse. Not now."

"Then what is it?" Her question touched the heart of the matter.

"It's therapy. Grief therapy. It's the only thing he's interested in. I've talked to his teachers, Anita. They say he's just been going through the motions, getting by. It would be a shame to lose him, but unless he finds a way out of his sorrow, he's going to sink beneath it." *Like Marco,* he wanted to add, since he'd asked around about the boy, but didn't. Jack was impulsive too often, but he wasn't stupid!

How could being near Jack's broad shoulders and deep rich voice make her feel so safe and secure? How could he make her forget Marco's complaints and remember Jesse's joy?

She sighed quietly. "I love my brother and I want him to be happy, but I'm responsible for him!"

"And you're doing fine, Anita."

It was nice to have someone reassure her, even another amateur. Maybe that's what Jesse got from his teammates: reassurance. She couldn't get through to him, but maybe some running around with a football could.

Anita nibbled her inner cheek.

Jack didn't want to push her, but... "Let him play half the game Saturday. If it helps him, he continues to participate. If not, he quits." Jack held his breath. She was putting them into an impossible situation, but what could he do? Walk away? From whom—her or Jesse? He needed one, the other needed him.

"Okay," she said finally.

Right there in the Dairy Queen, Jack kissed her. Swift and light, the kiss instantly ignited flames inside her. Jack's incredible effect on her libido still surprised her, but she was definitely getting used to enjoying it.

Giggling from the car next to them broke their embrace.

"Way to go, Coach!"

"Ms. Valdez is practicing her CPR," Jack said and the teenagers giggled again.

Anita glanced at them. It was Davey and Leo and Angie and Lisa—smiling, happy, lively. The way kids should be at that stage of their lives. It was her job to get Jesse back to the laughter, no matter what it took, no matter what it cost her. "I'll tell Jesse when I get home."

Jack reached down and turned the key in the ignition. As the engine roared to life, he waved his hand toward the school parking lot across the road and said, "I'll take you back to your car."

"Yeah, Coach—it's darker over there, anyway," one of the kids called as they left.

Jack pretended he didn't hear them. Did they think he was senile? He knew that! He wanted to kiss Anita without an audience. He might get impatient with her overprotectiveness, miffed at her questioning of his intentions and hurt by her disapproval of his chosen occupation, but one thing he never got was immune to Anita's sensual appeal.

In the parking lot, a good two hundred yards from prying eyes, Jack took Anita in his arms and kissed her thoroughly.

"Was that for letting Jesse play?" she asked in a dreamy voice when he paused for control. The night was silent except for some ragged breathing, and then he answered in that rich, soft voice that wrapped her in security like a fur blanket.

"Hell, no. When I kiss you—rockets go off when we kiss,

Anita. More than I want Jesse on the team, I want us to get to know each other and see if there's something more than this intense physical attraction between us. If there is, we can take it as slow as you want—but I can't walk away without knowing why kissing you launches those rockets." *Well, he knew why, but she needed to know.* "Will you give us a chance to discover what we could mean to each other?"

He held his breath as he waited for her answer. It seems to take forever when your future rests on one little word.

"Okay."

Jack breathed again.

"I guess we can date occasionally," Anita said, "but *I* make the decisions about Jesse. With no pressure from you—particularly this . . . sensual kind. It qualifies as undue influence."

Geez, she wanted the impossible! Then the tiny upward tilt of her mouth, the shimmer of her hair as it lay tucked behind her delicate ears, and the possibilities he saw deep in her eyes decided him. This was the woman he wanted. He didn't have to have her right now. He could wait until she was ready. He wasn't an overeager teenager, after all.

Besides, if he couldn't have her completely willingly, he might as well get used to the idea of celibacy. He didn't think he could settle for anything less than Anita Valdez.

"Agreed," he said. "Official weekly dates—and I get one good-night kiss per date." *Clever, Hayden. Frequent social contact. And where does one kiss start or end?*

"If you want anything more, you could try Rita Pawelek, Mary-Beth Sanderson, Leah Grona or Sue Hinojosa."

Jack stared at her as she rattled off the names. "Who the heck are they?"

"Eligible women in Larson between the ages of twenty-one and thirty—off the top of my head. I'm sure I can name four or five more if I think about it."

So, the tiny town was a hotbed of willing, single women. Another assumption about Larson bit the dust. Jack grinned. "Don't bother. This may be a casual, semiplatonic arrangement we're negotiating, but it's exclusive until further notice, okay?"

When she jerked her head up and down in agreement, Jack sighed with relief. Rearranging his knee forced him to stretch his arm across the back of the car seats. He grinned at Anita. "Wow, I haven't *dated* in years. This will be... rejuvenating."

If he crinkled his eyes like that every time he smiled, Anita was going to need resuscitating—her pulse was racing through her veins at stroke speed. "Just don't refer to me as your baby."

"Yes, ma'am. Sweetheart." Anita waggled a finger at him and looked at her watch. He reached across and opened her car door. When she slid into her own car, he said, "I'll follow you home."

Anita started to protest, then nodded. He was simply showing consideration, she decided, even if it was unnecessary.

It was nice having someone looking out for you. As long as they didn't take control.

Was that how Jesse saw her decision-making? She put the car in gear.

"Anita—thanks."

"For what?"

"You'll see." For making a novice coach's job much easier—and for giving him a chance at the happiness fame hadn't been able to give him, the happiness that ordinary people probably took for granted.

Should he tell Anita what he had in mind as the grand finale to their dating? A little proposal, a big wedding? Nah. She'd already made two commitments tonight. Probably all she could handle right now. And anyway, he figured he needed the element of surprise.

Chapter Six

To describe Jesse's reaction as "pleased" would have been criminal understatement. When Anita told him Tuesday morning that he could play half of the next game, he picked her up and swung her around, whooped "Yes!" and bounded down the hall with a huge grin on his face. Seeing the old Jesse again, Anita felt a surge of joy so deep, it rocked her as much as Jack's kisses did. So this was the power of maternal love? No wonder the race survived.

The first game was the main topic of conversation everywhere she went in Larson. Followed closely by Jack's coaching brilliance. And, of course, Jesse's contribution to the victory.

"Can you believe it? Four plays, four touchdowns. That kid is something else!" Anita heard that so many times, she thought an autopsy would reveal it engraved on her brain.

On Thursday afternoon, having missed lunch, Anita stopped at Smolik's to pick up a sandwich on her way to deliver an insulin pump to Ramon Hidalgo. While preparing her order, Vern informed her, "The coach ought to use

Jesse every possession this week. Those Beverley Bisons are tough—we can't beat them with just a running game."

Anita kept smiling, though she wondered if Vern Smolik was deaf. Didn't he hear her teeth grinding together? Variations of the butcher's remarks were all she'd heard for a week. The whole town was football-crazy. Apparently, they didn't mind letting their kids risk broken bones, spinal injury and brain damage if they could win a stupid game from another bunch of young, fragile, growing bodies.

What really bothered Anita was the knowledge that all she could think about, it seemed, was Jack Hayden, the sexy, sweet, goofy genius whose job it was to make these kids bang one another around.

Anita shook herself mentally as she paid for her sandwich. Jack wasn't Ivan the Terrible, intent on winning at all costs. He rested the boys when they got tired; he had Anita check each bruise and scrape; he never yelled at anyone—not even when that bonehead Aaron practically handed the ball to the opponent!

Jack had just patted the boy's shoulder and told him he'd learned a valuable lesson.

The conversation with Vern quickly lagged, since Anita had little knowledge of exactly how Jesse had scored so many touchdowns.

"Face it, 'Nita," she told herself as her little car hummed down the road to the Hidalgo ranch. "Jack's a good role model for the boys. And, personally, he's hotter than sin on Saturday night."

He was also the one person in Larson who didn't talk football. He always managed to be around at lunchtime, and before she knew it, he'd be asking about her patients or telling her stories about his wandering childhood. Or listening to her reminiscences as if all that dull stuff fascinated him.

Now, as she explained the pump's operation to Ramon, the dusky light reminded Anita of Sunday's dinner with Jack and their kiss afterward. The breeze was an echo of his mouth moving on hers, filling her with thoughts and feelings she'd never had. His kisses made her want so much....

Anita sighed. She felt guilty daydreaming about Jack when she had other things to think about. Like college for Jesse. Finding a way to move out of her uncle's house without hurting anyone's feelings. It was time to get on with her life; a permanent residence—in or near Larson—would symbolize the new phase.

Would Jack care that the past eight months had confirmed her deep desire to remain a part of Larson? The town was in her heart and vice versa. Maybe there wasn't any reason to think he cared. *Casual, semiplatonic.* What did that mean? The quicksand feeling was back!

"Okay, Anita. I'll try it to let you know."

She blinked at Ramon, one of the many diabetic Hispanics among her patients. He'd volunteered to be part of a study group.

"Uh, thanks, Ramon. If you have any problems with the questionnaire, just give me a call."

On impulse, Anita detoured to visit Marco Lopez before going home. When she found his room, the boy was moping, lying in bed facing away from the door. His mother apologized with an embarrassed shrug.

Anita shook away the apology.

Darn it—why couldn't things stay black and white? She realized it was the same thing—football—that took away Marco's laughter and gave Jesse's back. Jack's kisses made her feel safe and adored and powerful; his job made her feel scared and angry; his past made her feel helplessly overmatched. She didn't want to feel so pulled apart!

Taking a seat at Mrs. Lopez's request, Anita searched for something to talk about.

"How's Jesse?" Mrs. Lopez asked, then addressed her son, using a Spanish contraction of "my son" as an endearment. "You remember Anita's brother, don't you, *mi'jo?*"

The back of the boy's head nodded.

"Jesse scored four touchdowns Saturday." The words were out before she could stop them. Anita groaned inwardly.

Marco rolled over. "What position does he play?" he demanded.

Anita stared at the boy. He was actually interested in her answer. She didn't understand it at all. "Er, something called wide receiver, which is dumb because Jesse's as thin as a rail."

Marco pushed himself up into a sitting position, ignoring her little joke. "It means he sets up wide—away from the rest. Must be fast. Do they run mostly long patterns or short down-and-ins?"

Anita spread her hands wide with helplessness. "I don't know. Does it matter?"

Marco glanced at his mother before returning his attention to Anita. "Ms. Valdez, every single second you're really living, really feeling, experiencing something wonderful..." he glanced down at his legs "...you should enjoy the hell out of it, before hell is all you have left." Then he eyed his mother again and said sheepishly, "Sorry, Mom. I know I shouldn't say hell."

Anita barely heard his apology. She felt something wonderful every second she was with Jack. Would he leave her in hell?

Hollywood hunks don't stay in dead-end little towns, silly. He said he could take it for a year. He didn't say he'd like it. Her insides chilled.

When she said goodbye a short time later, Marco's mother followed her into the hall. "Your parents would be proud of you," she said softly. "Of the job you're doing here for all of us in Larson and for Jesse. I can see you're worried...." The older woman paused and looked down at her hands. "It's not my place to give you advice, Anita, but if your brother enjoys football, don't stop him. Everything happens for the best, you know. I believe that."

Her faith and acceptance were evident in her clear brown eyes. Anita pressed the woman's hands. "Oh, Mrs. Lopez, thank you for—"

"*De nada.* Thank you for coming to see Marco. It's good for him to be reminded that life goes on."

On the drive home, Anita's mind drifted. Marco. High-school students. Her own high-school days. Dating. Why wasn't she married, like most of her classmates? Because, romantic dope that she was, she'd never fallen in love. The most she'd felt for anyone she'd dated had been friendship. Even that doctor hadn't touched her heart.

Not the way Jack does, she whispered to the darkened highway. The way she felt about Jack Hayden—Anita had never felt this way before. It was something deep and swirling, something hot and soul-stirring. Just seeing his smile made her day better. Eating lunch with Jack made that bland school-cafeteria food taste like gourmet dining. He listened sympathetically when she shared the difficulties of juggling work with her new parenting responsibilities—somehow, his understanding made it seem manageable.

And his passionate kissing didn't hurt his case any, either! When his arms came around her, even when he brushed against her accidentally in the church nursery or the crowded hallways at school, her whole body tingled and ached for more.

It was a unique relationship, to say the least. On the subject of Jesse, she and Jack were practically enemies. The rest of the time, Jack could strip away her last brain cell with a wink or a smile, a sympathetic question or an understanding comment. Or a kiss.

Anita pulled into her uncle's driveway. That brought her back from the pleasant daydream of Jack Hayden. Her home was gone, so were her parents. Leaving her solely responsible for her brother. Her sense of inadequacy threatened to overwhelm her, but she was going to do her best to see that Mrs. Lopez was right. Her parents would be proud of her. And of Jesse.

* * *

Anita balanced her tray and looked for a seat in the crowded lunchroom. Scanning the crowd, she saw her brother, laughing and playfully shoving Danny. They were in the middle of a bunch of equally high-spirited boys, all football players, Anita noted.

She recognized a pang of jealousy, then. She couldn't remember the last time Jesse had joked or laughed with her. Their old easy relationship as brother and sister had been lost. If she asked him about homework, he got defensive. If she asked about practice, he got defensive. If she asked about anything, he got defensive. And she got defensive right back. Anita sighed.

"I'm not sure the school is insured for wind damage," Jack murmured, his warm breath tickling her ear.

Anita jumped, the dishes on her tray sliding precariously. "Jack! I didn't see you."

"Obviously," he agreed, herding her toward a vacant spot at the back of the cafeteria. "Hi, guys," he said as they passed the laughing boys.

"Hey, Coach," came the chorus.

"You were a little preoccupied with heavy sighing," Jack said as they set their trays down and pulled out the metal folding chairs. "Anything you care to share?"

When Anita hemmed and hawed, Jack settled his paper napkin in his lap and picked up his fork. "A motherhood problem?"

Anita looked across at him and couldn't help smiling. Could he read her mind or was this one of his heavy-handed innuendos? Jack was about as subtle as a freight train.

"I called you last night. Are you sure it's safe for you to drive alone at night? What if something happened to your car?" he asked.

Anita was cutting her mystery meat into minute pieces at record speed. It was the only sign she was agitated, but Jack had begun to appreciate her unspoken messages even if understanding them didn't come naturally to him.

"I have a CB in my car and I know every person and every road in the county. And I... Never mind. I'm perfectly capable of driving at night without an escort." She speared a piece of meat and lifted it to her mouth.

"Your car isn't the newest thing on the road, Anita."

"What did you call about?" she said, changing the subject.

Jack shrugged and said, "I called to talk. Isn't that allowed when two people are dating?"

"We talk every day, Jack."

He made a great show of looking around the bright, crowded, noisy room. "Yeah, we talk. In public, for public consumption. No opportunity for secrets."

Anita grinned at his disgruntlement. "Just what kind of secrets do you have?"

Jack thought about it half-seriously. His volunteer coaches had made enough jokes to make him realize his entire playing career, including his idiotic remark after the Super Bowl, was public knowledge in Larson. He didn't have a chance to create any new secrets since he couldn't get Anita alone for more than five minutes. Sadly, her idea of dating lacked a solitude factor.

"None. I lead a blameless, boring life. They're going to nominate me for Boy Scout of the Year."

His mock distress was so comical, Anita found herself laughing. He could do that so easily—make her forget her worries. It was as if Jack were the sun shining down on her life, filling it with warmth and light.

"Seriously, Anita, there are times when Larson is too darned small."

Like that, the sun disappeared. Black clouds rolled in, but she wasn't going to let Jack see them. It was an inappropriate reaction, anyway. After all, Jack leaving Larson—unattached to anything or anyone here—was probably inevitable. Look on the bright side. Maybe once he was gone, she could talk some sense into her star-struck brother without Hollywood interference.

"Well, if you're bored, move on."

"Anita—" He looked confused, then retreated behind a polite mask she hadn't known he possessed. "I have a contract to coach football and teach at Larson High. It expires next June. I can look for another position after that."

She stood up, her lunch half-finished. "Sure. In a bigger town. More money. More attention. That's all you care about, isn't it? Endangering the lives of youngsters to make yourself successful! Well, go ahead. My brother's too naive to understand what you're really after, but I'm not."

Anita turned and ran out of the lunchroom. Jack watched her go, frowning, frustrated, confused and helpless in the face of her outburst.

He wadded up his napkin, dropped it on his plate and pushed his chair away from the table. He was facing an impossible situation. Learning a new job, trying to help a talented kid find his bearings again—and falling for a wonderful, caring woman who disliked him for doing it. Combine the mental seesaw with a large dose of physical frustration and . . . "Sh—"

"Better watch that, Coach." The advice came from his biggest player, Greg Pawelek. "Wouldn't want to ruin your nice-guy image."

Jack's muttered suggestion about what could be done with his image left the student speechless as he watched the coach stride jerkily out of the cafeteria—in the opposite direction from Nurse Valdez.

"Why aren't you at the pep rally?" Anita asked when Jesse appeared in her office as the last bell rang. She'd been hoping Jack would stop by and insist she go to the rally with him, but he hadn't shown up. She couldn't really blame him. After all, she'd yelled at him right there in the cafeteria!

Jesse lifted one shoulder and dropped it, without ever removing his hands from the pockets of his jeans. "Why bother?"

"Jesse, the team—"

"Who cares about the team? If I get a little bruise, you'll make me quit, so why bother. I'll quit now and avoid the rush."

What had gotten into him? Anita frowned. She was really too inexperienced to parent a teenager. She needed to start small and work her way up. Her brother's mood swings—were they normal adolescent rebellion? Grief? They'd always been so close, but now she sensed Jesse was holding something back. Anita wished she could tap Jack's store of male wisdom right now—she was thoroughly stumped.

"Jesse, I'm just concerned about your safety. About your future."

"You treat me like a baby, 'Nita!'

"Jesse, please—" Taking a deep breath, Anita apologized. "Jesse, I'm really trying to do what's best for you, but you're right. I don't always know what that is."

His hands still in his pockets, Jesse sagged against the door frame and stared down the hallway outside Anita's office, not looking at her. That, too, was becoming familiar.

Anita wanted to pull her hair with jealousy and frustration. Instead, she clasped her hands on the desk and asked quietly, "Jesse, what do you think Papa and Mama would have done about this football stuff?"

The boy looked at his shoes until he seemed to have the raw pain under control. Anita was slower with her own.

"Papa let me play last year. And he sure didn't interfere with the coach's decisions about how often to play me."

He actually took a step toward Anita. "Don't you realize your limits just make me a target? If I only play a little, the other team knows Danny's going to throw me the ball, so they'll double or triple-team me. I'm more likely to get hurt that way than playing all the time."

Anita stared at her hands, dodging the yearning in her brother's eyes, but she couldn't ignore his logic. It was probably just as true for half the game as it was for four plays. Jack had known that all along, she realized. He'd tried to tell her that, in fact, but he hadn't pushed her. He'd respected her right to make the decision. *Believed she would make the right decision.*

The awareness made her... Geez—now he could make her tingle in absentia!

At last, she nodded. "Okay, play as much as Jack wants. Go down to the pep rally and tell him I said so."

"Uh-uh, Sis," Jesse said with a flash of white teeth. "Coach won't believe me."

Anita smiled back, realizing that she'd just given herself an opportunity she was too smart to pass up. "Then come on. I'll tell him in person."

Of course, she hadn't really expected Jack to pick her up in front of the whole school and plant a swift but sensational kiss on her willing mouth before twirling her around and then staggering like a clown under her apparently excessive weight. It was, Marci gushed afterward, a fabulous way to end the pep rally.

Larson was too small to bench all the starters in the fourth quarter, but Jack pulled Greg, Jesse and Danny out when the score got completely lopsided. Anita smiled when he looked over at her, obviously hoping she'd be impressed by his clever strategy of taking her brother out of the game without injuring his pride.

The smile was all the encouragement he needed, thank heavens. Jack sidled up to her and murmured, "Let's ditch these guys after the game and go someplace where we can be alone."

One of the players ran by and jostled them together, pushing Anita into his hard chest. His arm came around her instinctively. Protectively. When she shivered with the reaction to his touch, his arm tightened around her in glorious response.

Anita had gone into nursing because she loved medicine and liked taking care of people, but that didn't mean she didn't enjoy receiving a little caretaking herself. *Mmm—imagine playing doctor with Jack!*

"I'll bet we end up at the pizza parlor with a horde of boisterous teenagers," she predicted with a smile that told him that was okay and eyes that said she wanted some privacy.

"There's always our date tomorrow night," Jack growled deliciously in her ear before returning to his strenuous duties of walking out onto the field for the post-game handshakes.

Part of Jack's success in sports was due to his great peripheral vision. Exchanging cordial remarks with the opposition at midfield, he could still keep track of Anita. Of course, the radar he'd developed about her helped even more than the peripheral vision.

He was tuned in to Anita Valdez, turned on by Anita Valdez and hog-tied by her, as well. He had some great game plans worked out that he couldn't use because they might really put Jesse at risk. It was too bad; Jesse was exceptionally talented and the plans were brilliant—well, he had to do something while Anita gallivanted off to deliver babies or save lives.

Didn't she realize how rare their kind of attraction was? How it should be cherished and nurtured? Probably not—after all, she'd been lucky enough to be normal all her life. She couldn't be expected to understand a military brat whose family moved constantly, who had to make new friends every few years and learned to put on a cocky front, when all he wanted, like everyone else, was to be accepted as he was, warts and all.

Jack turned and walked back to his own side of the field, steeling himself to face the crowd of well-wishers converging on the team—and him. This was one of the things about professional sports he hadn't cared for, an invasion of privacy he'd fought until a veteran player told him to view it as the cost of doing what you wanted to do. "Everything has a downside, Hollywood," Leon had said. "Just to balance things out."

So Jack put on a smile and politely accepted the attention and congratulations, until he realized that this was different. He knew the name of every person he talked to, knew their kids, where they lived. And they knew him. Unlike the fans in Los Angeles, these people would offer the smiles, the handshakes, the pats on the back whether the team won or lost.

"Good game, Jack. Say—Bubba said your car's leaking a little oil. Bring it by the shop Monday, I'll take a look at it."

"Thanks, Ned. I'll do that." These people took care of one another. Which reminded him... "You seen Vern around?"

Ned Johnson snorted and pointed. "That's him in the crazy hat. Claims it's lucky."

"Whatever works," Jack said, noting with complacency that Anita had slithered away while he refocused the congratulations in the team's direction. *Larson's too small, woman,* he told her silently. *You can't hide. Not from me.*

"Vern—got a minute?" It *was* a crazy hat, but who knew. The team was undefeated so far. Eight more to go. And then Jack would have more time to chase Anita, if he hadn't caught her by then.

"Great game, Coach."

Jack started. He'd lost himself in a fantasy of making love with Anita. Luckily it was dark—too dark for Vern to see him blush. Jack scrambled rapidly through his memory to discover why he'd hailed the butcher. *Oh yeah.* "Vern, you know Raul Obregon?"

"The kicker?"

Jack nodded, then Vern did, too.

"He told me he might have to quit the team. His dad's out of work temporarily. Hurt his back. The family—"

Vern interrupted, assuring Jack that he'd give the boy a job "mopping" the meat, which he explained was a vital step in producing the barbecue Vern's family had been selling from the back of the meat market since 1912. He waved away Jack's heartfelt thanks.

"Anything you need, son. You'd better scoot now. Anita's looking to make a getaway."

Vern caught Jack's elbow and steadied him when he lost his balance spinning around to follow Vern's pointing finger.

"You okay, Jack?"

"Yeah—it's... Old habits are hard to break. Sometimes I forget I'm not perfect anymore."

"The kids think you are. Do you realize they've already won as many games this season as they did all last year?"

"They're older, more experienced," Jack muttered. He wasn't going to take any credit. He still had a lot to learn. "Some of them were playing the wrong positions, too."

"Okay, Jack, whatever you say. Get going or you'll lose her," Vern said, giving him a little shove and laughing.

Jack hurried across the gravel parking lot, praying his knee wouldn't give way on the uneven surface.

"Anita, wait!" He was almost there. A breeze brought her perfume his way. Was the woman trying to drive him to an early unconsummated grave? That perfume of hers seemed to penetrate to his very core, until he could swear he smelled those spring flowers in his dreams. He felt beads of sweat forming on his upper lip remembering the content of those dreams.

She turned and her hair swung past him. He grasped a strand of the shiny black silk and pulled her gently toward him. "Aren't you coming with us for pizza?"

Anita studied him in the cool light from the security lamps. Those toasty-warm eyes were as clear as well water. The heat she always felt was flickering through her insides with those half hopeful, half anxious looks. Who could resist this hunk with the little-boy gazes and the sexy body and the gigantic heart?

"Sure." The boys idolized him and so did the town. Maybe she did, too. Grades were up, discipline problems were down—and Anita's libido was stuck in high gear. "Sure. Pizza."

"And a real date tomorrow night," his deep voice promised. "How about dinner at my place?"

"In that case, I'd better fill up tonight." She grinned, as another storm of tingles swept through her. Dinner at his apartment. And dessert?

She'd read about some truly wicked uses for whipped cream.

Anita spent Sunday afternoon mowing the long grassy meadow between the highway and the house. She maneuvered the riding mower automatically while her mind drifted. She'd heard about Jack's arranging Raul's employment with Vern. Did Jack see that's what made Larson such a special place to live or did he think it was all his doing? Was he trying to fit in or take over?

She wondered again if Jack was really what he seemed to be; wondered if Jesse would come out of his troubled grieving; wondered if Marco would ever make peace with his disabled state. They were unanswerable questions that lost their urgency in the September sun with the smell of new-cut grass in her nostrils and the memory of Jack's spine-tingling, bone-melting kisses still in her heart.

In the shower, Anita caught herself humming the latest country hit. She was happy because she was looking forward to seeing Jack again, she realized, and she realized something else: it—no, *he*—was the first thing she'd looked forward to in a long time.

When she arrived at Jack's apartment, Anita knocked and heard a muffled direction to enter. Not long ago, Jack had made a comment about people around here leaving their doors unlocked. Comments like that weighed against his generosity in helping Raul. If only she could be sure how he really felt about the town. Did he like Larson or barely tolerate it? Did he miss the city the way she'd missed her hometown? Was he Hollywood Hayden or Jack?

Either way, she'd better lock up her heart, because he hadn't made any promises. *What promises did she want from him? We're only investigating an attraction,* Anita reminded herself, then pushed open the door and went in.

The living room had been painstakingly cleaned. The kitchenette was open to the front room and her first view of Jack was a profile: he was bent from the waist, peering anxiously into the oven. His narrow hips and powerful legs were encased in khaki slacks. She knew the dark green shirt he wore would deepen his eyes to a dreamy forest shade and set off his still-gorgeous tan and his muscular upper body. Anita felt her pulse speed up—nobody in her own world had ever affected her the way this "interloper" did.

Their first meeting flashed through her mind. Even her deliberate inattention had been unable to dilute Jack Hayden's powerful sensual effect. She remembered that the air had been charged with energy the minute he walked into the picnic tent. *Just like now.*

"Anita, honey!" His smile of welcome drove the room temperature up five or ten degrees. "Have a seat and relax," he said. "I'll be out in a minute. Can I bring you something to drink?"

Darned if her ornery little mind didn't populate a penthouse with starlets hearing the same question. A small-town nurse competing with that kind of glamour—she was nuts! She wasn't even in the game.

Hayden was clattering pans in there like a one-armed short-order cook. He'd consulted her about the menu at church, then headed full speed for the big grocery store in Kenedy.

Anita put aside her uncertainties. Tonight, Hollywood was here. He'd invited her to dinner. She intended to enjoy it.

The evening flowed like ribbon cane syrup—slow, rich, deep-flavored. Not that the meal was exactly up to anyone's gourmet standards: the rice was sticky, the vegetables were almost raw and the meat was a little dry and tough, but culinary standards were of secondary importance.

The main course was Jack Hayden. While they ate, he kept up a steady flow of entertaining conversation, teasing her whenever possible without mercy—and without malice. He drew out her opinions on the subjects they discussed, and when they occasionally disagreed on something, even Jack's dissent took an agreeable form.

And speaking of form... Every inch betrayed his magnum-force masculinity. Apparently, Jack didn't need to act hostile or aggressive or tough for him to feel like a man—he let his physique take care of that job. With a body so unrelentingly male, his behavior could be charming, sweet and kind.

When dinner was over, he put a tape into his elaborate stereo system and joined Anita on the sofa. A soft country ballad filled the air. "Thanks for dinner, Jack," she said, letting a hand rest on his muscular forearm. "What's for dessert?" Her eyes fastened on his mouth of their own accord.

"Strawberries and cream," Jack answered, his eyes so easily read. "Unless you have a better idea...."

Her mouth fit his perfectly. *Would everything else fit as well?* she wondered dazedly as passion rose between them as hot and swift as ever. Boldly, Anita moved against him. She wanted answers. It was research time! "Touch me, Jack," she whispered.

He groaned softly as his hands slid around her waist, gently tugging the material of her blouse away from her skin and slipped beneath it. His hands moved slowly upward, and when he cupped her breasts and stroked her sensitive nipples with his callused thumbs, she thought she knew what those romance novels were talking about. Pulsating clouds of passion, spiraling pleasure. This was definitely the best lovemaking....

He distributed kisses democratically along her jaw and down her neck. A few swift movements and Anita's blouse fell open. Jack's mouth continued downward to the edge of her bra, then traveled slowly over the thin lacy covering.

As the aching created by his caresses grew stronger, deeper, more delicious, she murmured her jumbled thoughts aloud, "I was mistaken. It gets better and better."

All Jack heard through his own fog of passion was the "mistaken" part. "Oh, gosh! Anita, I'm sorry, I'm sorry! I—I got carried away. You're so beautiful, so made for loving. I couldn't help myself—I mean, I should have. No! That is, I shouldn't have—" Even as the words came tumbling out, Jack was rebuttoning her blouse, smoothing her hair, drawing her into a sitting position.

Tidying up. She pushed his hands away. "It's okay, Jack." She tucked in her blouse quite thoroughly to cover her embarrassment. She'd thrown herself at him; he'd declined. "My fault."

"Are you... Are you really upset?" The words were so pathetically anxious and those big eyes were filled with—Was it possible to fake such concern? Was Hollywood Hayden that good an actor?

"Don't worry, I won't tell the Booster Club." Anita busied herself fiddling with her collar while she tried to manufacture some strong emotion—indignation, or something—to balance the still-raging desire this man evoked in her. Sure as shooting, nobody's touch had ever seared her soul like that before. To be honest, she wasn't nearly as humiliated as she was shamelessly wanting more! "Just tell me why you stopped."

His eyes widened. "You said it was a mistake, so I..." He shifted forward eagerly. "Hmm. Come here, woman. I'm sure I can find my place again if you'd like to resume our activity."

"I'm not sure that's a wise idea." Anita held her hands up, palms outward and Jack sat back. "Maybe it is time I went home. Larson might begin to wonder what's going on here."

One corner of Jack's mouth lifted. "This town knows by dawn what you dream at midnight. I'm not worried about what the town thinks, but I promised you I'd behave like a gentleman and here I fall all over you like a starving man on a feast. I'm sorry, Anita."

"Don't carry the noble-gentleman malarkey too far, Jack—I might start thinking you're getting your...

satisfaction elsewhere." *Or that you're carefully avoiding entanglements.*

"You know better than that, don't you?" He was sitting on the edge of the sofa and his voice vibrated with concern. Honestly, you'd think he was seriously worried! Did he really care that much about her answer?

"Yes," Anita said, and then smiled. It was true. Rita Pawelek and every other eligible woman in the county would give their eyeteeth for a night with Hollywood Hayden, but you could tell by looking deep into his eyes: he wasn't that kind of man. Jack might head for a bigger pond soon, but he didn't break hearts just for practice.

My gosh, Anita, do you really think this football coach could be the one decent, compassionate, sensitive, sexy man left in America? Then why would he stay in Larson? He's right, after all—it's a darned small town.

"How about those strawberries now?" he asked.

At her jerky nod, Jack unfolded himself from the sofa and got busy in the kitchen. Anita knew he was giving her time to put herself back together physically and psychologically. Add thoughtful to his list of virtues. And extravagant—strawberries were not in season in September.

"How much did the berries cost you?" She lifted her voice so he could hear her over the mixer whipping fresh cream.

"If they make you happy, they were cheap."

She didn't trust herself to stay much longer after that. She was either going to decide he was the biggest fibber in the universe—or she was going to pull him down on the sofa again and discover the truth about the fit of his trousers.

Either way, she was getting in way too deep to get out without somebody's getting hurt. And that somebody had a brother to think about and a hometown she didn't want to leave again. If anybody asked her to, which they hadn't.

Chapter Seven

Three weeks later, Jack considered asking for a rent rebate. His landlord had to be saving a bundle on hot water with all the cold showers Jack was taking!

All this self-control! Am I eligible for sainthood yet? Jack wondered as he slid a tray down the lunch line. Three weeks of dating Anita Valdez and Jack was about as head over heels as possible. And he couldn't do a thing about it. She'd retreated after that dinner at his apartment. Made sure their activities were exceedingly public, kept conversation light and meaningless and paused only for too-brief good-night kisses before disappearing into that darned crowded house. He wasn't making any progress that he could see.

Which brought him to the other end of the seesaw: football. The Badgers were still undefeated and the topic came up too frequently during their public encounter-dates. He was beginning to see why some people actually hated the game. It interfered.

They couldn't seem to talk about Jack in the present tense without bringing up his occupation, then Anita's ambivalence appeared. And then Jesse usually got dragged into it, which brought dangers—real or imaginary—into the conversation. It wasn't exactly the stuff of courtship.

He'd tried, very carefully, to bring up the future in general terms, but Anita didn't want to talk about it. And frankly, he was too afraid of getting a flat, bridge-burning rejection to push the issue. The past—well, *nobody* wanted to talk about the recent past.

Jack set his lunch tray down on what had become "their table" and contemplated his fortunes, hoping Anita wasn't out on a call. Was he ever going to be alone with her again? Could he propose on the basis of a few kisses and hope she got over her lingering prejudice against him and his calling?

Because coaching wasn't a job anymore, or even an occupation. It had become a calling. Jack sighed. Even if Anita eventually accepted the concept, he doubted she'd be happy about the salary. Unless he left Larson, he'd never be able to support a family lavishly. The way Anita and a couple of babies—say, a dozen—deserved to be supported.

Anita knew there was more to life than money, though, didn't she? As Larson coach, Jack was making a difference. Greg Pawelek wanted to play for Coach Hayden badly enough to master geometry after failing twice. Raul Obregon could stay in school and support his family, thanks to Jack's intervention with Vern Smolik. Not that Jack had gotten Raul the job, but he'd been able to open the door for the boy.

Coaching the Badgers fulfilled him; he couldn't give it up, but he wanted Anita, too. He wanted her to be happy with him. If he had to make a choice... Jack put his chin in his hand. It was a lousy dilemma.

"If you're bored, Rita can be here in ten minutes." Anita pulled out a chair and set her tray down next to his.

Looking deeply into her velvety brown eyes, Jack could have sworn they were alone, not in a noisy school cafeteria. "I couldn't be bored around you. What'll we do Saturday?"

Anita looked at his smiling sexy mouth, his hard healthy body and tried to remember her resolution not to get involved any deeper. The more she thought about it—and his background—the more ridiculous it seemed to imagine Jack staying here, teaching at Larson High year after year. He had no ties here; he was used to big cities and to moving around. She couldn't hold Jack here any more than she could deny Jesse what was important to him.

She'd thought it out carefully, made up her mind to break off this silly, dangerous dating before anyone got hurt—and what happened?

The same thing that always happened: Jack's eyes twinkled and he smiled and she forgot all reason, responding to his endearing personality and ruggedly masculine charm like a mindless lump of female flesh.

Hours of excruciating mental effort down the tubes and she didn't even care.

You're crazy, she told herself, but self wasn't listening. Self was smiling like an idiot at Jack, who was saying, "The Floresville Peanut Festival is this weekend. We could go to that, if it's not too sophisticated for me."

Anita scraped off a layer of bemusement and looked closely at that seemingly open face. Had Jack finally learned sarcasm?

"I'll show you the ropes—you'll get the hang of it." A clump of kids walked by, greeting the coach and the nurse.

Watching their progress across the cafeteria over his shoulder, Jack said, "I'm excited about Greg."

Anita picked out the Pawelek in question. "What about him?"

"He's finally passing geometry, but he's having trouble with chemistry and he needs it to graduate."

"So what are you going to do about it, Coach?" The challenge in her voice indicated that some antagonism still simmered just below Anita's delectable surface. Jack wracked his brain, but the only difficulty he could do anything about right now was Greg's.

"I think I'll ask a brilliant EMT I know to tutor him one afternoon a week during study hall. With my awesome persuasiveness, she's sure to agree."

"I think you're going to be the main exhibit at the Peanut Festival," Anita said, wrinkling her nose. There was something awfully cunning about Jack's candidness.

"I feel like an idiot," Jack said Saturday night, his arm nonchalantly draped around Anita's shoulder. A huge stuffed purple rabbit dangled from his hand. "How'd you learn to shoot like that?"

Anita raised the small glass bowl she held. "How'd you learn to throw like that?"

"Answer the question, sharpshooter."

With those dark eyes, she slanted him the look that made him burn late at night. "It's not very liberated, I'm afraid, but Papa refused to let me train as an EMT until he knew I could take care of myself—we answer calls twenty-four hours a day."

Jack wanted to enjoy the feel of her against his side, but for once his brain was working.

"What?" The image shocked him. Tiny Anita—armed and dangerous. "You carry a gun?"

Her slow smile almost turned him inside out. "This is Texas, Jack. Weapons are part of the lore. Look around. Every pickup has a gun rack—very few hold umbrellas. During hunting season, you'll see more rifles around Larson than in some of those Central American civil wars."

Jack shook his head and chuckled. "I can't get over this place! Pistol-packing county nurses. Peanut Festivals with queens and parades." He laughed and waggled the purple bunny. "If my old teammates could see me now, they'd never believe it."

"Sure they would."

Oh, boy. Her eyes were flashing.

"Hollywood Hayden Amused by Podunk Celebration."

"Anita—" Now what the heck had he done? "I'm having a great time. Come on—I'll win you another goldfish."

"Look, Jack, I know it's just a corny little festival, but it's good, clean family entertainment. You don't have to ridicule us for—"

"But I'm not! Honest, Anita, I—"

Just then, Jesse, Danny and Bubba came screeching to a halt in front of them. The crowd on the midway split and flowed around them.

"Hey, y'all! Who won the bunny?"

Jack waggled the toy at Anita. He'd removed his arm from her and stepped a proper foot away, but the boys were grinning ear to ear, their eyes darting from the coach to his girlfriend. "Deadeye Valdez," Jack admitted. "You boys having fun?"

"I thought you were supposed to be home studying," Anita's sharp voice broke in, reminding Jack of his mother. He grinned involuntarily in sympathy with the boys, then tried to produce a stern, adult face. *Obviously, she'll have to be our kids' disciplinarian,* he thought—and grinned again.

"Aw, Sis—gimme a break," Jesse pleaded. "It's Saturday night. I'll study tomorrow—"

"Tomorrow! All your talk of wanting to be an engineer—if you don't keep your grades up, you won't even be able to attend the local junior college."

"I'm not going there!"

"Jesse—"

"This isn't the time for a lecture, honey." Jack put his hand on her waist and applied gentle pressure. Jesse's face was clouding up, his lips tightening, his eyes shuttering. Anita's expression was a perfect match. *So the stubbornness was genetic.* Jack stepped between the two.

"Jesse, you know studying is important, but it *is* Saturday night. You and the rest of the guys have fun, but I want you on the road home by midnight. And tomorrow, you hit the books long and hard, okay?"

The boys nodded vigorously and scattered before the coach could change his mind.

After a moment of tension-filled silence, Anita apparently decided to ignore Jack's interference this time and turned toward the food booths lining the fairgrounds where this year's Floresville Peanut Festival had again drawn a record crowd. "Maybe I'll just kill him and save the cost of tuition.

"It's hard to remember being that young and carefree," she went on. "I need food after that—and don't call me honey in front of the kids," she added without pause.

Also without heat, so Jack simply said, "Yes, ma'am," and dug some money from his pocket.

"Tell me something, Jack," Anita asked a minute later as they waited for their corndogs-on-a-stick. "Are you flattered when kids leap to do your bidding?"

"Flattered?"

Anita tossed her hair at his apparent bewilderment. "Just answer the question. Honestly."

"Honestly?" When she nodded, Jack decided three weeks of treading water was all he could stand. Somehow, he had to move Anita past whatever stumbling block she'd erected. Too bad it was going to involve *talking.*

"If I can nudge a kid in the right direction, I will. Yes, it makes me feel good. My revered position as football coach gives me an advantage around here. I'd be irresponsible not to use it positively."

She was supposed to be impressed by his altruism, but she was decorating her corndog with mustard and didn't have time.

They strolled the festival grounds slowly, eating their corndogs in the glare of the flashing lights of the carnival. Then they wandered through the exhibit tents displaying award-winning peanut-everything. As they reached the last mound of peanut brittle, Jack placed a finger under Anita's chin and lifted her head until she looked into his eyes.

"This festival's been fun, Anita, but please—do you think we could go someplace quiet now and talk candidly?"

"About what?"

"About what's really bothering you. Is it Jesse? Or us?" Jack took a deep breath and let it out slowly. "Or me?"

Those eloquent eyes say he understands Jesse—and me. They say he cares, really cares about us both. Despite an urge to tremble, Anita managed to smooth her hair rather than display her vulnerability. "What's there to say?"

"We made a deal, Anita," he reminded her. "We agreed to find out if there's more than simple physical attraction between us. After almost a month of dating, I think it's undeniable. We also agreed to decide what to do about it—and we can't decide anything with these obstacles between us."

"Obstacles?"

He looked as if he wanted to swear, but he merely said, "Jesse. My job. Your job. Your fears. Peanuts. I don't care which one we pick, but let's talk about one of them."

"My fears are reasonable," Anita insisted.

Jack's finger traced the outline of her lips. "Maybe they are, but there are always going to be problems to face. Why can't we handle them together? I want to share everything with you, Anita."

Oh, she was tempted! Since the day they'd met, Jack had been darned-well seducing her with his considerate behavior, his friendly Boy Scout act. Making her feel safe and sure with his reliability. Working his way through the anger and pain surrounding her heart with the sweetness of his devotion. Those brief but thorough kisses he planted on her each time he took her home burned away whole forests of fear. *Face it, woman, you'd like nothing better than to share your burdens with this broad-shouldered master of masculine charm. But how long would he share them before handing them back—along with your broken heart—and loping off to civilization?*

"Well . . ." Maybe it was time to get some things out in the open. To know whether there was any chance for her and Hollywood Hayden to find common ground. She might as well face the truth before the quicksand sucked her completely under. "I don't think the peanut brittle wants to hear this."

"Then let's get out of here," he said in that deep voice that melted another layer of resistance each time it flowed over her.

It wasn't the intimate locale Jack would have chosen with a first pick, but the monument in the center of the Larson town square was where they ended up. It was neutral and safe and, at eleven o'clock at night, deserted.

Anita perched on the ledge surrounding the engraved nameplates; Jack sat on the step below and stretched out his leg. He rubbed the sore knee absently as he pondered how to approach a delicate topic.

You have to think this time, man—your future rides on overcoming her objections, whatever they are, without trampling her feelings. It was easier said than done, of course, especially for Jack, but what he felt for Anita made him determined to try.

"So, which problem shall we solve first? Jesse's future?" he asked gently, letting the night carry the question to her. One weak spotlight cast distorting shadows over the small plaza, making it seem less real and, he hoped, less threatening. He knew some of her concern and he had some ideas on the subject, but he wanted to hear her version.

"We talk at practice," he continued. "Your brother's got big dreams, but he knows there are problems making them happen."

Anita sighed. "It's no big deal, really. Everybody raising children faces the same stuff."

"It is a big deal, Anita." The conviction in his words dissolved more self-doubt. "Just because it's common doesn't make it less important. Air's pretty common, but it's darned necessary."

Anita smiled, but her nerves were fluttering. She had some wild hope that this would bring them closer together. Of course, she was probably nuts to expect understanding from Hollywood Hayden but she heard herself explaining.

"Look, Jesse's obsessed with being an engineer. Has been ever since I can remember. Every kid deserves a chance at his dream, but there isn't an engineering program available nearby. He'd have to go away to school. With three incomes, we might have managed, but they—when they—"

Jack covered her hand with his as her voice wavered and broke. Her fingers tightened in his and her narrative resumed. "My parents didn't have any insurance, their only asset burned. Jesse gets social security benefits, but that's hardly enough to buy books."

Anita pulled her hand free. "I'll be lucky if I can afford to send him to the local junior college. And Jesse's so stubborn—he says he won't go there."

"You'll still have transportation costs, books, all that—even if you can persuade him."

"Thanks for reminding me," Anita said heavily. "I know what Papa wanted for Jesse. I want it, too, but I don't know how to make it happen."

"Honey, we—"

"Jack, I...I can't be anyone's honey. Jesse's my first responsibility. My personal wants or needs have to come second." In the half-light of the square, Anita's face said she expected him to walk away.

Is that what she thought of him? That he couldn't be bothered with what bothered her? On second thought, maybe he was selfish, thinking only of his own fulfillment here in Larson. Any woman wanted her man to want to give her the moon. What would Anita's opinion of Jack Hayden be if she found out how unambitious he was? It would probably drop lower than it already was.

Jack stood up, automatically compensating for his knee's buckling when it first took his weight. "Anita, do you have to do this alone? Is it some kind of female macho thing? Personal definition, or something?"

"What are you talking about?" But a smile threatened.

"Could I help with Jesse?"

"Jack, you're an underpaid teacher, not a wealthy philanthropist. What can you do?"

He extended his arms horizontally and pivoted like a mannequin on display. "Anita, you see before you a man who's made a few enemies and a lot of mistakes—except that it all worked out for the best, I hope."

"What are you talking about, Jack?"

His hands dived for cover in his pockets and his wide shoulders scrunched together. "I think I still have a few friends left."

Anita sat in the monument's shadow, her head tilted to one side.

Jack reached across the intervening space and stroked her full lower lip with one trembling finger. "I came to Larson to put the past behind me," he said softly. "So that I could move forward. I want you, Anita. I want us to move forward together. Brother problems and all."

Anita's lips pressed against his finger, then her breath shuddered over his hand. "Oh, Jack..."

The sudden movement sent searing pain through his knee, but Jack didn't care as he closed the space between them. Then his arms were around Anita, drawing her into his chest, pulling her body between his thighs. His head bent and his mouth devoured hers with a hunger that demanded...everything.

And Anita wanted to give everything. Wanted to forget her problems and their differences and lose herself in the spiraling desire his lips, his tongue, his hands created within her.

It was more than sensual desire that fueled her fiery response, that sent her hands sliding over his broad, strong back, that inhaled his scent of spice and musk and soap and sun, and insisted that her tongue explore his taste, his mouth. It was more than lust that wanted to give to him and to take...everything. Anita jerked her hands away from the top button of his cotton shirt. What in the heck was she thinking of?

She was thinking of falling in love with Jack Hayden. Love! Love? Anita's mind raced with her pulse. Her heart tumbled senselessly out of control.

"I want you. I want us to move forward together."

She'd wanted to hear that first sentence, wanted to believe it. But the rest... You couldn't move forward without leaving something behind. Jack wanted to leave Larson. It wasn't a surprise; the surprise was how much the declaration hurt. Because—how could she go?

"What's wrong, Anita?"

"Nothing, nothing." She slid a finger under her hair and tucked some loose strands behind her ear in a nervous gesture. "It's, uh, getting late." As though on cue, a night bird emitted a few mournful notes. Anita's hands went to her arms, rubbed up and down once. "Getting cool, too."

After a pause, Jack accepted the change of subject—and activity—with a regretful shrug. *One step at a time.* "It's October...." He offered Anita his hand as they descended the monument steps, then bent and unlocked the car door.

"The farmers say this'll be an early winter."

"Anita." Jack interrupted her weather-logue. "Anita, we don't have to figure it all out tonight, but I *will* help you with Jesse. And we'll work out everything else that keeps us apart. The only thing I want between us is a little piece of paper."

"A piece of paper?"

"A marriage license."

Damned if her stomach didn't turn flip-flops of anticipation instead of knotting with regret! "A marriage license, Jack?"

He didn't mean it, did he? Her head whirled. She couldn't think right now! She needed time and space.

Selecting a light, joshing tone, Anita said, "Give me a break! You'd never survive the wedding—not the way we do 'em around here."

Jack put his hands on his hips. His legs were slightly apart for balance, but it was a pure warrior's stance and Anita's own knees threatened to buckle at its display of male power. "You might not survive the wedding night, Ms. Valdez! I'm an incredible gentleman with unbelievable control, but I have to tell you—it's not natural. Not around you." Jack's growl sent delicious, aching shivers through her from head to toe.

"And I'm telling you, you'd never make it that far," she managed to say finally.

After a hot, challenging look, he silently handed her the goldfish and helped her into the car. When he slid behind the steering wheel, he said, "Okay, what's so special about Larson-style weddings?"

"Irene Delgado and Joe Janek are getting married in November. Come and find out."

"I wouldn't miss it for the world," Jack assured her with a grin. "Is Joe related to Elly? Probably. I love weddings, don't you? Hmm... I have a nice dark wool suit if it's cool enough. Shows off my broad, manly shoulders." Anita was shaking her head. "What?" he demanded.

"Jack, check the map. This is Texas. You're the only man this side of San Antonio who wears polished loafers and pleated slacks. They look nice on you, don't get me wrong." *Hell, a burlap bag would look nice on that body!* "But you're in a different league now. Different uniform. Think now, honey—who were the girls draped all over tonight at the festival? What were those ol' boys wearing?"

How could he think? How could he remember how to walk or swallow or breathe when she called him "honey" with laughter dripping down her voice. He wanted to lick the corners of her mouth, then slowly work his way down her throat, past that little hollow at the base of her neck, then... He yanked his mind to attention; his body was on its own. "Let's see—the drapers wore tight jeans and puffy bangs. How were the drapees dressed?"

"Like cowboys, Jack. Girls around here like cowboys. So that's what you're going to see at Irene and Joe's wedding—cowboys decked out in their finest hats, boots and jeans. Two-steppin' around the floor—"

"I get the picture." He interrupted her descriptive monologue. "No suit—too formal. No athletic shoes—too sticky for sliding. Jeans and leather soles." It was too dark to see it as they pulled up in front of her house, but she could hear his smile.

Did he find Larson's informality amusing? Had he enjoyed the festival tonight or thought it pathetically unsophisticated? Was there hope he could adjust to Larson's style and pace? Did he want to? *I want to move forward.*

"I can't wait, Anita. I'll take lots of mental notes."

His kiss was undeniably full of promise—and weakness flooded through her. Was Jack Hayden serious about making a commitment to her or just the world's greatest kisser, who could wipe out her common sense with the move of his mouth on hers? "See you in church very soon," she said, easing from the embrace and indicating her watch. It was way after midnight.

Jack groaned theatrically. "What are our chances the Burnses' baby teethes at home this week?"

"Slim to none, honey."

Honey. As he headed home, Anita's swift kiss burned on his cheek and the image of the perpetually crying Burns child was replaced with visions of another baby. One with shining black hair and big hazel eyes....

Since they'd made so much headway Saturday night—mostly through what wasn't said, like *get lost, Jack*—Jack was able to handle the bawling Baby Burns good-naturedly. He was a little upset not to find Anita home Sunday night, but Jesse informed him Monday that there'd been a wreck out on the highway with minor injuries and chickens everywhere; Jack decided to be understanding.

He missed her Tuesday, too. She was gunning her engine and heading south when he limped to his car through the lunchtime rain. Jack prayed briefly that the call wasn't serious and that Anita would arrive in time. Maybe it was the Jackson baby finally putting in an appearance.

He watched her taillights disappear and tried to be realistic.

There was still a lot to resolve with Anita before he could hope for his own dreams of marriage and family to come true: her doubt, fear, grief, duty. All tangled up with her need to love, her hunger for passion, her desire to give as well as receive.

Practical considerations, too.

If he could convince her that love mattered more than money, if he could solve her brother's college problems, if he could cure Marco's paralysis—would she focus all that passion and love on him? Well, he'd conquer these things the same way he'd led his team to the Super Bowl: by following a carefully constructed game plan, one play at a time.

Jack headed the little red car out of the parking lot and three minutes later limped up the sidewalk to his apartment, glad he'd brought the car since the rain had settled in. His mind still focused on Anita. He knew he was lucky to meet the woman of his dreams, attracted first by her dark, romantic looks, then coming to love her for her caring nature, her intelligence and her loyalty to a traditional life-style and values.

For weeks now, he'd been a good knight—carefully wooing his chosen maiden, demonstrating what a wonderful catch he was, controlling the passion she roused in him.

There were dragons in the picture and Jack hoped to defeat them with the power of his devotion. He knew it was too simple to be true, but darn it—it *ought* to be that simple. He'd come to Larson, found a job that satisfied him and met Anita. What more could one want out of life? Jack thought it should be happily-ever-after time.

It wasn't that easy, though, and Jack was feeling helpless. And yes, a little angry. And pretty frustrated, too.

He loved Anita—that came from his very bone marrow, but patience had never been one of his virtues. He felt like a boxer in the final round of a championship bout. His stamina was gone; fatigue—mental, physical and emotional—had Jack on the ropes.

How much longer would he have to wait for Anita to decide he was too fabulous a deal to pass up? He had a birthday coming soon—he didn't want to wait forever to be married, to love Anita completely and, hopefully, to father a child or two. "I'd like to have a baby while I'm still young enough to remember its name," he muttered, wincing as he took the last step. His knee was throbbing today—nothing helped in this weather.

His neighbor poked her head out of her doorway. "You're home kind of early, aren't you, Coach?"

"Yes, Mrs. O'Brien," Jack answered politely. "That is, I'm just home to use the phone. The school district won't pay for personal long-distance calls." He smiled at the elderly lady. Burglars with a professional interest in his stereo were out of luck even with his door unlocked; they'd never get past Eagle-Eye O'Brien.

Jack knew it was expected, so he asked about her cat, then excused himself and went into his apartment. As he picked up the phone and began dialing, he eased down into a chair. He needed to surmount at least one of the obstacles that stood between him and his goal. Maybe this—if it worked—would convince Anita once and for all that Jack Hayden was too good to let go. Or at least that he meant what he tried to say.

Jack listened to the clicks as the call went through. He didn't want to do something stupid, but the man running out of patience was also grasping at ideas. If he couldn't completely vanquish Anita's concern over the drawbacks of organized sports, maybe he could balance it with a really impressive display of the benefits.

When he cornered Jesse with the results of his phone calls, the boy's vehement response surprised Jack. "Forget it, Coach. Sis is talking about making me quit the team again. Says I got my priorities screwed up just because my physics teacher, Mr. Jenkins, gave us a pop quiz over stuff he hadn't even covered yet and I blew it!

"I think she's the one who's screwed up!" Jesse's outburst continued. "She used to be a pretty neat sister. She's been a pain in the—a real pain. But now she's acting like... like a psychopath!"

Jack cooled Jesse down by promising to handle Anita. *How?* After searching frantically and unsuccessfully for her Wednesday morning, Jack modified his game plan, adding a risky, go-for-broke play. Why not? Unless it worked, he probably had nothing to lose. He spent that evening on the phone and then on the road.

Thursday, he cornered Anita in the cafeteria and herded her with his tray toward their usual table. "Hi, George," he said automatically as they passed a group of laughing boys. "Danny, Jesse, Bubba, Tony."

Anita chose the last chair on one side of the metal and Formica table. Jack sat across from her; there were a few vacant chairs between them and some middle-school teachers. It was as private as things got at Larson High. Anita was frowning in the direction of the boys they'd passed.

"They're just having a little fun." The giggle level was exceeding the norm. "Besides, tomorrow's Homecoming. And I have a surprise for you. At least, I hope I do."

No response. His nerves fluttered. *Maybe he'd take the long way....* "You missed a good meeting Monday—the boosters really let me have it."

Well, that got a little interest. "About what?"

He tried to spear a potato slice with the dull cafeteria fork as he mentally prepared his story. He'd discovered with delight that yarn-spinning was an art form in Larson and he'd been studying the masters: Vern Smolik, Gus Pawelek, Elmer Wiatrek.

"When I first drove into Larson," he began, momentarily abandoning his potato chase, "I was shocked, Anita. Disappointed. I couldn't believe how small it was. I thought it was too small for *any* of my purposes. Too small for a decent football team, too small to contain any eligible women... But I thought it was just the right size for me to achieve my number-one goal, which was to escape my reputation as a playboy jerk."

Anita had dropped her fork and was glaring at him. Well, it was a reaction.

"You came here looking for single women?" she whispered, furious. "What the heck for? Oh, that's a stupid question! Oooh!"

Finally capturing and consuming the wild potato, Jack grinned at her irritation. That was hopeful, wasn't it? She felt something for him—he only hoped it was enough.

He held his hands up in surrender. "Anita, wait. I'm just telling you I came here loaded with assumptions about life in small towns. The citizens of Larson, Texas, have blasted all of them to smithereens. Number one, I met you—not just any single woman. You."

Jack went on before Anita could protest, but not before her rising blush gave him a rush of pleasure that would have been highly visible if he'd been standing up. "Number two, I'm working with some of the finest players I've ever seen. Jesse, Danny and Bubba have real potential. And last, but sure as heck not least..." He started laughing helplessly. As usual, the warm sound melted Anita's burgeoning resistance like sunlight banishing frost.

"This town—*everybody* in this town—has known all about me since day one."

Anita looked at him, nonplussed. "What did you think?"

Jack choked back the laughter. "I thought in such a small town, my past would be a secret. I thought it *was* a secret—nobody ever mentioned it."

"Oh, Jack, get real. Of course, we knew all about you—including that dumb remark you made!" And then she quoted it to him, " 'I'd rather wrestle a cobra in a barrel of roaches than get married.' "

He stared at her. "The exact words. You really knew."

"Jack, we do have television in Tinytown! It all got rehashed when you were hired." Anita shrugged. "Nobody around here could see why we should judge a man on five seconds' worth of reaction to a nosy, irrelevant question. Did you really think it was a secret?"

Jack nodded sheepishly. What he'd thought was his lucky escape from the past turned out to be Texas-style good manners. "When somebody at the Booster Club questioned my intentions toward you and I insisted I was holding out for marriage—they really let me have it. The quips started flying every which way like those white-wing doves you showed me." His eyes were twinkling with remembered glee.

"You find this funny?"

Jack actually laid his head on the table beside his tray for a few seconds of helpless laughter. "Yes. You see, I came to Larson because... I had no place else to go." He sat up and leaned toward her. "Anita, I tried three different jobs in three different cities in three years. Each time, some media type resurrected all that old immature behavior, including that quote. The exposure created such a negative atmosphere that co-workers, acquaintances, even strangers turned against me. Nobody said it was old news, forget it. Nobody gave me a chance to demonstrate it wasn't smoking-gun proof of a malicious personality."

Anita shook her head firmly. "You're not malicious, Jack. You may talk before you think, but your heart's in the right place."

For a long moment, Jack just beamed at her, then he reached across the table and clasped her hand. *Was it possible to receive redemption in a high-school cafeteria?* Somehow, he'd expected trumpets and fireworks, not kitchen clatter and cabbage smell. "Thank you, Anita." He made himself remove his hand and curl it around his milk. "That's what they told me at the meeting, too. More or less." He chuckled again at the memory.

"More or less?" Anita prompted, when he appeared to lose his train of thought in apple brown betty.

"Well, they told me my heart was in the right place, but they also told me my head was up my—"

"Jack!"

Cocking his head, Jack tuned his eyes to unbearably endearing level. "I'm sorry, Anita—I'm verbally clumsy. It's my biggest handicap."

That charming ineptness is no handicap and you're about as resistible as a teddy bear. "You're a nut, Jack Hayden."

"Yeah, but I'm cute." He grinned to demonstrate. "You know, that ribbing they gave me at the Booster Club meeting—it meant a lot to me. It meant the people in this town accept me."

"I think you could say they even like you," she agreed dryly. "If you keep winning, they'll canonize you."

"I'll admit the team's success helps my reputation." When the smile died and the shuttered look covered her eyes, Jack sighed. He wanted to reach across the table and plunder her mouth long and deep. Instead, he dug his spoon into the dessert and asked a question he didn't want to ask.

"How are you and Jesse getting along?"

Anita's upthrust chin declared her stand on the subject. "He's acting like a child, so I'm treating him like one."

Chapter Eight

Her dusty-rose, vaguely uniformish outfit flattered her profoundly, Jack noted as he wondered how to respond. The subject of Jesse always meant trouble. His best player had also unwittingly become his worst enemy. Jack, who wasn't naturally cynical, refused to appreciate the irony. For a moment, he hesitated, torn between ethics and personal gain.

She'd already told him to mind his own business. But he'd promised Jesse an ally.

"You two squabble like a couple of toddlers over a toy," Jack blurted out and groaned. Even he knew you didn't criticize people you were trying to woo.

"Jack!" Anita sputtered.

He started babbling, hoping to repair the damage somehow. "You spend more time worrying about a perfectly normal kid than you do about all your patients combined. Or me."

Anita started to argue with him, then paused. Why, Jack sounded almost jealous! A spontaneous thrill went through her and she forgot to be appalled by his assumption that she was interested in his opinion of how she ran her family.

You're thrilled that he's jealous of Jesse? she asked herself silently and decided she must be as goofy as he was.

That wasn't all they shared. In addition to that goofiness and the incredible physical attraction that sang between them, they had similar tastes and goals; they both loved helping people.

Too bad their backgrounds were so different—along with their plans for the future. Jack's talk of a marriage license... Anita had already figured out that had been an unconscious reversion to an old habit—automatically putting out the kind of bait a naive, romantic woman would fall for.

No need for bait, Jack. I think I'm already hooked. Anita wondered how painful the process would be when he threw her back. Would she be strong enough to heal her wounds? Or did she want to be a "keeper" if it meant living in an alien environment. *I could, but do I want to—even for Jack?*

"You never have time for me, for us. I mean, I'm trying to be understanding, Anita, but I'd much rather... Oh, forget it."

Jack raked his hand through his hair and Anita almost smiled. He *was* jealous—of her brother—and he felt awkward about it. He seemed so easy to read! Anita liked the idea of knowing where she stood.

"Anita, I'm not asking you to neglect your responsibilities. In fact, I'm trying to help, but you're not helping me help!"

"And you're not making any sense," she replied a little defensively. "As usual. If you're referring to my latest wrangle with Jesse, I suggest you butt out. I have certain standards about grades and priorities that I will not compromise. Jesse knows what they are, too. He chooses the consequences of not complying with those standards."

Gosh, she sounded like such a prig, even to herself!

She forced herself to calm down. *He probably didn't mean to sound critical,* she told herself and smiled. "Look, Jack, you gave the lecture about preventive measures, remember? That's all this is."

"Preventive measures?"

"Seat belts?" she prompted. "Eating pizza with the team after the game—what is that but baby-sitting to keep the celebrating within safe limits? Threatening to bench Jesse is the same thing."

She wanted him to get back to the part about "time for us," but his next statement blasted the thought out of her head as fast as a politician forgets his campaign promises.

"Threatening Jesse with the loss of something so important to him is not good parenting."

Now, *that* was criticism!

It took every ounce of Anita's self-discipline not to sweep her tray and dishes onto the floor. "Important? Bad parenting? What the hell are you talking about?"

"That physics quiz was a minor grade. He's still got an A average in the class."

That slowed her down. "He does?"

"Yes, Anita, he does." Oh, Jack's eyes could look so reproachful. "You overreacted. I recognize the symptoms. Believe me, I'm an expert at it."

"Overreacted?" If she mouthed the word softly enough, she might not grab him by the tie and shake him.

"Did you or did you not tell Jesse he couldn't play this week? We need him."

The last of her hopes plunged. She was a first-class fool!

"So that's what this is about! I should have known. You don't care one bit about Jesse. You don't even care about me—you just want your star player on the field to make you look good. Why? Got a line on a new job and need another victory to cement the deal?"

Those warm hazel eyes turned to cold jade. She'd never quite realized just how strong and firm his jaw got when he got mad or how. . . *big* Jack Hayden was. Anita swallowed hard.

Jack pushed his tray aside with one shaking finger. "I'm not building myself up at the expense of children's lives, Anita," he said in a voice like frozen steel. "But I need to know if... if Jesse will be available for the game tomorrow."

"I'm not sure." She didn't care if she sounded like a petulant child. "He's got an English test this afternoon and that grade *is* borderline. And he came home from practice limping last night. It's just a sprain, but I'm not taking any chances."

"You're taking a chance with his future."

"What do you mean?" Her eyes fastened on his mouth. How could she be remembering the taste of his kisses when they were arguing!

Jack clasped his hands on the tabletop in front of him, kept his eyes on them. "A friend of mine will be here tomorrow, specifically to see Danny and Jesse play," he said. "Dub Collins is the head coach of my alma mater—who just might be willing to recommend awarding full four-year scholarships to both boys. If he can see them play."

Anita jumped to her feet, her head reeling with implications, hopes, dread. That university had an excellent academic reputation. A full scholarship! But four more years of worrying—and long-distance, too. She'd be completely gray-haired before graduation. *But an engineer...!*

"Don't you dare tell Jesse."

"Sorry. He already knows." Jack stood up, too, towering over her across the Formica. "And so does Danny. Those two are a pair, Anita. They need each other to showcase their abilities for Coach Collins. So your decision affects Danny's future, as well."

Anita said a very unladylike word under her breath. She threw her hands up in a gesture of defeat. "Okay, you win. I'm tired of fighting everybody. I'm tired of Jesse hating me for trying to take care of him—"

"He's seventeen, Anita, not seven. It's time to care *about* him, not for him."

"And I'm tired of my parenting being critiqued by inexperienced bachelors—"

"That's your fault, too, Anita. I'm ready to change that status any time you say the word." He was looking straight at her, straight into her heart with eyes that were warm again and willing and wanting.

She stared at him for the space of five or ten or a thousand heartbeats. "Are you proposing in the Larson High cafeteria?" she asked softly.

"Anyplace you want. Name it."

"I—but we were arguing, Jack!" She shook her head dazedly. "Talking to you is like waltzing with a hurricane."

"Speaking of waltzing, will you go to the Homecoming dance with me? I volunteered to chaperon, just in case you'd come. I'll bet we could manage a few dances between rounds of policing the punch bowl."

Anita spun away. She waved once, feebly, without looking back, already halfway across the cafeteria.

A student ambling past said, "Don't sweat it, Coach—at least she didn't turn ya down."

Jack looked at the retreating student and shook his head ruefully. Compared to courtship in Larson, the media attention at the Super Bowl was a closed-door, secret meeting.

The erratic Texas weather cooperated with Larson's Homecoming. Autumn arrived right on time with crisp, cool, perfect football weather. At game time, Jack stood on the sidelines in his lucky navy blazer, a sweater underneath, as the Fighting Badgers lined up to face their archrivals.

The stands were packed with fans ready to shout and cheer at the slightest provocation; the players were bouncing up and down on the balls of their feet as they waited for the opening whistle. He thought back to the seconds before his Super Bowl game began: the tension had been no higher then than it was here and now, on a patchy field of dried grass on the edge of Larson, Texas. Jack grinned in anticipation. This was better, so much better.

He looked down the side of the field—Anita was actively not meeting his eyes but Jesse was suited up and ready to go, one perfect English grade under his belt. Jack glanced at the red-hatted figure in the sea of blue: Dub Collins had arrived as promised.

Jack gave his lucky blazer a pat.

If he could help Jesse achieve his dream of studying engineering at a first-class school, maybe Anita would see that his "dangerous" sport offered wonderful opportunities to talented, needy students like Jesse and his friend Danny.

And if tomorrow night worked out as planned...maybe she'd be so impressed, she'd answer his proposal with the right word.

The boys came through with some spectacular plays. The pride Jack felt for their performance was ten times greater, ten times sweeter than his own success on the football field. "This is where you belong, Jack Hayden," he muttered to himself as the clock ran down. "Larson High, not Hollywood. Here's where you can make a real, lasting difference. Here's where you matter." The picture was only missing one piece to make it perfect. If Anita Valdez would agree to be his wife, Jack would be completely happy.

Jack clung to the student's remark in the cafeteria: she hadn't turned him down yet. And he had one more trick up his sleeve.

When the clock ran out, Jack and the team did their handshake routine at midfield, then returned to a swarm of hometown fans congratulating their winners. He wasn't surprised by Anita's conspicuous absence. His abrupt announcement had been blunt and tactless, as usual, but he'd wanted to be sure the scholarships were real possibilities before he raised anybody's hopes.

Jack found Dub Collins and, after a back-pounding reunion, introduced him to Danny and Jesse. Leaving them to get acquainted, Jack worked his way to the locker room, where he praised the team for their teamwork and great play. Then he and Dub reminisced until the last boy had showered, dressed and primped himself into presentable shape. When the teenager left with a tired but happy good-night, Jack snapped off the lights and locked the gym. Dub paced him as they began the trek across the parking lot to Jack's car. Jack moved slowly; the hours of standing in the cold night air had taken their toll on his knee.

After a good-natured night on Jack's sofa, Dub made breakfast. Then they picked up Jesse and went to the Paweleks' house to discuss the boys' educational future in Indiana.

Jack excused Anita's absence by saying that she'd been called away on an emergency. He calmed Jesse with private assurances that his sister needed a firm scholarship offer before she'd seriously consider letting Jesse go so far from home.

Jack sincerely hoped he was telling everyone the truth—especially when Dub clapped him on the shoulder and said, "Hollywood, you were right about these two. Look forward to coaching them. Something else I want to mention—there's gonna be a position available on my staff next year. Just an assistant slot, but it's a step up from high school. More money, of course."

"You want me, too?" Jack was astonished, flattered—and torn.

"How could I break up such a beautifully matched set?" Dub asked, spreading his hands and looking appreciatively at Jack and the two boys.

Jack got Dub on the road to San Antonio to catch a plane back to Indiana. Then he laid out his clothes for the dance, now just a few hours away. Stepping into the shower, he started to get seriously nervous.

Regardless of what happened tonight, if he couldn't persuade Anita to let Jesse accept Dub's scholarship offer, his big plan was a flop. Jack was counting on Anita's gratitude being the extra nudge that pushed her over the threshold into loving him. If it backfired, he might lose her permanently. Have to leave Larson, all his dreams shattered.

He'd take Dub's coaching offer if Anita wanted him to. Probably she would. Every kid couldn't count on a full scholarship and there were so many things to provide before college....

Jack rubbed a hand over his chin and got dressed. He had one last rabbit to pull out of his hat. If it worked the way he hoped it would, Anita ought to be thoroughly convinced of his value to Larson, to humanity, and—oh, please—to Anita Valdez.

If it blew up in his face, however, he was dead. Plain flat busted. Finished with no time left on the clock to try again.

It had to work.

Anita stepped into the shower Saturday night with a sigh of relief. She let the warm water flow over her tired muscles, willing them to relax, willing herself to rejuvenate.

She hated farm-equipment accident calls, but thankfully, this one hadn't been as awful as it sounded when it came in. Tom Ehrens would miss the first joint of his finger, but the shredder could have taken off his arm—would have if his five-year-old hadn't followed directions so quickly and shut off the machine.

After showering, Anita blow-dried her hair and dressed quickly in a rose silk dress she'd been saving for some special occasion. A heated confrontation with her brother wasn't exactly the special occasion she hoped for, but—*Darn Jack Hayden! It's all his fault.*

Anita applied a little makeup, hoping Jesse would be gone before she finished. She didn't want to fight tonight. It was Homecoming. Time for fun. Music and dancing. Jack.

As she manipulated the clasp on a thin gold necklace, Anita rehearsed her arguments again, just in case. Jesse had come home from the Paweleks' on cloud nine. "I don't think—" she'd begun and he'd stormed out, returning at dinnertime.

Probably went to enlist his coach's help. Anita speculated on Jack's probable approach, then gave up. He was too unpredictable. *If he kisses me, I'm a goner,* she admitted. *But what a way to go!*

She left the bedroom and there was her brother, slumped on the sofa, watching TV.

"Why aren't you dressed, Jesse? They present the Court at nine."

"Who cares?"

Anita put down her purse carefully. She would remain calm. She would try, once again, to reason with him. "Jesse, you were elected to that Court by the student body. You're expected to be there."

"So what?"

Anita counted to ten. She. Would. Remain. Calm. She'd be mature and rational. "So get dressed!" she shouted.

Jesse jumped to his feet, eyes blazing. "Stop telling me what to do! You've already ruined my life—you think—so why don't you just shut up and leave me alone?"

Anita was speechless. Thank heavens the others were gone already. "What do you mean—I've ruined your life?" she finally managed to say.

"And Danny's!" Jesse was still shouting. "His parents won't let him go by himself. The engineering program's fantastic, too, but you won't even listen to the guy—"

"Danny's parents should make their own decision, I agree." There. That was reasonable. "I'll speak to them, but you're not playing any more stupid football!"

"You just don't get it, do you?" Jesse asked hotly. "I *like* football. Out on that field—everything else goes away. For those few minutes, my life's . . . like it used to be."

And I worry about you every second.

Jesse jammed his hands into his pockets. He looked steadily into Anita's eyes. "I *am* playing football, 'Nita. Danny and me figured it out. We're going to Indiana. I'm getting my engineering degree—all paid for."

"I absolutely forbid it!"

Jesse gave her a funny smile and his next words hit her like hammer blows. "I'll be eighteen in March, Sis. I won't need your permission. I told Coach Collins I'm going. And you know what else? Coach Hayden's going with us. Coach Collins offered him a job that he'd be crazy not to take."

Jesse stomped out of the room and a moment later Anita heard the shower start. She remained motionless, facing a number of cold, hard facts she didn't want to accept.

Undoubtedly, she qualified for Idiot of the Century! She'd screwed up everything. Forced her brother to choose between football and her—and he'd chosen sports. She couldn't blame Jack Hayden for this fiasco. All he'd done was give Jesse those moments of peace on the field and a way to have his dream.

Anita bowed to the inevitable and picked up her purse. She'd better ask Jack about this Indiana coach and the school he represented. And about his job offer and whether it included a marriage proposal. Anita swiped at some stupid tears. Jack made her tingle, but Larson made her feel safe.

A strange town, filled with strangers. Cold ones, maybe. Different habits and food and... And four more years of worrying about Jesse.

Anita went outside and ran down the porch steps. Right now, she needed some familiar faces—and one in particular. She hoped he'd be glad to see her.

Jack's reaction to her arrival was everything she could have wanted. He turned and his smile grew positively radiant. He immediately excused himself and began walking across the gym floor, oblivious to the people around him; he only had eyes for Anita.

The rest of her planned agenda vanished when she looked past Jack. The person he'd been talking to was Marco Lopez, wearing a tie, shoes and streamers of Larson blue woven through the spokes of his wheelchair.

"Anita, you look absolutely exquisite!" Jack's big strong hands engulfed hers, the contrast of rough skin against smooth sending icy-hot tingles right through her shock. The depths of his eyes were warm and willing, even in the semi-darkness of the gym, which had been decorated, though not transformed, with crepe streamers and honeycomb paper ornaments. His smile made her heart pound.

What was Marco doing here? She told herself there must be some logical explanation. He was talking to, and smiling at, one of the cheerleaders. Lisa. Anita had the sinking sensation that Jack had something to do with this... whatever *this* was.

"Okay, okay—it's only one man's opinion. Maybe you only look fabulous?" Jack was still smiling but a little furrow of worry wrinkled his forehead.

"Thank you, Jack." She tried to act as if nothing was wrong. "You look handsome yourself this evening." He wore his high-fashion, Hollywood look: pleated pants, a pink dress shirt with the sleeves folded back and a very MTV-ish tie.

"What's Lisa doing with Marco?"

Jack glanced over, shaking that little wayward strand that was always falling on his forehead in an extremely sexy way. "Talking to him. Did you know they were an item last year? Went together or whatever they call it now."

Anita tried to say something appropriate but only managed a weak, "Did Lisa invite him?"

She knew he was going to smile that sheepish little half smile. She knew he was going to say, "I thought it would be nice for him to get out, so I called his mom and she helped me arrange it."

Anita couldn't respond. He thought he was being kind, but his impulsive behavior could so easily seem cruel. Didn't he ever stop and think? How could a person hope to interpret him accurately or know where they stood with him?

Jack pulled her onto the dance floor as the deejay started another tape. "Come on, honey. They're playing our song."

"What song?"

"One we can slow-dance to."

Anita let him lead her around the crowded gym. She was reeling from too many shocks in rapid succession. She needed Jack's strong arms around her to hold at bay some thoughts she was trying not to think.

As the song ended, he loosened his embrace enough to satisfy public opinion on proper teacher conduct. Barely. Anita leaned back to look up at him without leaving the circle of his arms. *It's nice to have such strength supporting you sometimes. Especially tonight.*

Jack's fingertips moved in tiny circles at the small of her back. "I had no idea the nightlife around here could be so wild and wonderful," he murmured, pulling her closer again.

"This is the wildest thing you can imagine—slow-dancing?"

Jack's lips curved in a sleepy, suggestive smile that stirred her insides into that wanting state that made her crazy for something she couldn't even name. He shook his head slowly. "I spend hours imagining something much wilder and much sweeter . . . with you. The way you make me feel, Anita, I could *easily* be convinced to ditch my noble principles and do some horizontal dancing with you."

Her eyes told him more than the curve of her lips dared. The fire he saw there held enough heartstopping promise to strengthen Jack's resolve. He'd hold out for total commitment. Anita's values were as traditional as his own. Without a wedding ring on her finger, she might come to his bed, but she wouldn't stay.

He pulled her close as the music started again. "Let's dance in that direction," he said, indicating a corner of the gym. "It's darker over there."

But nothing lasts forever, including dance music.

When the song ended, Anita unerringly spotted Marco across the crowded gym and headed in his direction.

Jack followed slowly. His plan was to somehow make Marco an ally, but now he felt a surge of pure panic that it was going to backfire. Anita had probably known this kid since he was in diapers; he'd surely back her opinion of Jesse's scholarship. How could a newcomer compete with lifetime ties?

Anita bent to greet Marco, smiling at him, then turned her head toward Jack and let the smile die. She touched the boy's arm. It was a familiar, protective touch and it turned Jack's insides into a sheet of brittle, rusted-thin iron, flaking into the dust of broken dreams.

He'd come to this town as a last resort. They'd taken him in, accepted him, given him a chance to start over. Knowing Anita had given him a chance to experience what few people are privileged to know: true, deep, always-and-forever love.

Maybe she didn't share it yet, but she felt *something* for him. Jack's rusted-iron will turned to cold forged steel. He wouldn't give up what he'd struggled and searched and yearned for, not without a fight. He took a step toward Anita, then another.

He ordered his knee to behave and with two more long strides he was there. Jack looked at Lisa, then at the pouting boy in the wheelchair. Rock music thundered from overworked speakers, but Jack's heart outthundered the music.

"Come on, honey—let's show these kids how to fast-dance." *Oh, good move, goofy! Act insensitive to Marco's limitations. Stir her sympathy. Why not just hand her a rope, then put your head in the noose?*

Marco's eyes widened and his mouth fell open. "Lisa said you were something else, Coach Hayden, but I didn't know what she meant."

Jack remained silent as the pout reappeared on the kid's face. Then he waded in with both feet to try to save his busted play. And to escape his panicky feelings.

"I hear you and Lisa were close last year."

"That was before."

Oh, Jack remembered using that sullen tone. So he mimicked his physical therapist. "Before what?"

Marco produced an odd crackling noise. Anita's hand rose to her lips and she said, "Let's talk about something else."

Lisa stepped around to stand beside Jack, facing her wheelchair-bound former boyfriend. She put her fists on her hips in perfect cheerleading form. "Okay, Ms. Valdez. We'll talk about something else. I know. Tell me why you broke up with me, Marco. I always wondered."

Marco stroked the armrests of the chair, then pounded them with his fists. "Come on, Lissie—no girl wants a boyfriend who's a cripple."

Lisa put her cute face close to his. "How do you know?" she demanded. "Did you ever ask me?"

"I didn't have to. That stupid tackle ruined my life."

Jack studied the boy dispassionately. He'd been angry like that once, but his therapist had coolly pointed out that he had the power to choose whether his injury was going to be a stumbling block or a stepping stone.

He glanced at Anita. She looked as if she'd turned to marble. Jack muttered one of those words he shouldn't use. His brilliant plan was a failure, mangled like a spiderweb swept into a shapeless clump, and he couldn't stop it, couldn't repair it. Didn't even know exactly what was doing the damage.

Something snapped inside him. Enough was enough. If Anita would rather cater to Marco's blatant self-pity than understand what Jack was trying to do, she'd never love him enough.

So, with nothing left to lose, he decided to set the kid straight. "*You're* ruining your life," Jack said, using his frustration to fill his voice with contempt instead of sympathy.

"Football crippled Marco," Anita argued hotly. "Naturally, he blames it for—"

Jack stared deeply into her eyes, trying to find something that maybe had never been there.

"Football didn't cripple Marco. And neither did I."

"You're talking nonsense, Jack. Or should I say, Hollywood?"

He ignored her question. "No, I'm finally making sense. It's not where you're from or what you do or what happens to you that matters, it's your attitude about it."

"Easy for you to say," Marco muttered.

Lisa punched Marco's arm. "Oh, shut up, you big lug, and listen to him. Your mom told me your doctor thinks you might be able to walk again if you'd work harder."

Anita and Jack faced each other, the kids forgotten for the moment.

"Look, Anita, you pull people from car wrecks. It's dangerous—"

"I'm helping people, Jack!"

Her implication was a slap across his face.

"You think I'm hurting the kids on my team?" he asked softly, like the glint of moonlight on a knife blade. "That's what you think of me?"

Anita caught her lip between her teeth. Before she could answer, Marco broke in with another self-absorbed comment, "Well, look what happened to me."

Jack turned on him, his dreams drowning beneath waves of hopelessness. "So what?" he barked.

Marco blinked; the color drained from Anita's face. Jack became resigned then. He'd wanted to bring things to a head; now he had to finish what he'd started.

He'd lost Anita, anyway. Maybe he'd never had her.

"Do you think anyone gets a guarantee from life?" he asked Marco, capturing the boy's full attention. "Well . . . ?"

Jack glanced around at the avid faces of the crowd that was suddenly surrounding them. Oh, great, a big public scene. Again. He hadn't even noticed the music ending and all of Larson approaching to catch the performance.

Jack gazed at Anita's still-frozen expression. Apparently, he hadn't noticed a few other things, either, blinded by his own dreams. It looked as if he didn't need to take Dub's job offer since he wasn't going to have a family to support. He could stay in Larson the rest of his life and eat his heart out. Well, everyone needs a hobby.

Breaking the silence at last, Marco blurted out the question that Jack knew was festering inside. "But why me? Why did this—" he gestured at his paralyzed legs "—happen to me?"

Putting his hands on his hips, Jack studied the boy for a moment, then said matter-of-factly, "Why not you?"

He heard Anita gasp, but Jack kept his eyes on Marco as he explained gently. "It's a useless question, son. The answer won't change anything. It happened. This is the way things are now. You just have to get on with your life.

"Ms. Valdez here lost her parents in a tragic accident. Is she standing over the ashes of that fire, crying and moaning?" *Figuratively, maybe.* "No. She's trying to move ahead, to build on what she has left. You ought to try it, kid, instead of holding a continuous pity-party, trying to make everyone else feel guilty because they're paying their own dues, not yours."

He turned to Anita. "I'm sorry, honey, but if you can't see how much I care for you and Jesse, if you can't see how destructive Marco's self-pity is, if you really think my goal in life is to ruin young kids' lives..." Jack lifted and dropped one massive shoulder. "I guess there's nothing more to say." He spun on his heel and disappeared through the crowd that was frantically pretending they hadn't witnessed anything.

Anita helped Lisa bundle Marco into the van Jack had arranged for the boy's transportation. She caught snatches of "...call me..." and "...working hard." She gave them the shortest polite farewell in history; it was all she could manage. The two kids were too immersed in each other to notice, anyway.

Anita was never sure how or when she got home. She'd driven for hours, but it hadn't helped. Jack's words had hit her with the force of an avalanche.

The last few hours before dawn, she lay awake facing another new reality. It was all over. Jesse would get his chance. Marco, too, was on the road to recovery. And Jack had his ticket out of Larson. She'd lost her brother and Jack all in one night.

As she lay there listening to Letty mumble in her sleep, she tried to follow Jack's advice: she didn't ask why. He'd changed his mind, that's all. It didn't matter if it was over Marco or Jesse or because that job offer gave him a sure way out of Larson. Plenty of single women in Indiana, that's for sure.

She shouldn't have read so much into a casual mention of a marriage license and a half-bored semiproposal in a school cafeteria. She shouldn't have believed what his eyes seemed to say.

Maybe she'd never known the real Jack Hayden. Maybe all she let herself see were the things that made her fall in love with him. Like the way his kisses burned like starfire. The way his eyes warmed when they saw her. The way his smile smoothed out the misunderstandings of his impulsive tongue. She remembered the wonder on his face when he'd held Dale's newborn baby, the confidence he imparted to his players.

His players. That, too, was something that had no special reason. It was just a fact. Jack was a football coach. A talented one with plans for his own life. Plans that apparently didn't include her. A strangled, semihysterical giggle escaped her lips. She'd been worried about staying in Larson, safe in familiar territory, rather than risk competing with the rest of the world for Hollywood Hayden's affection. She'd wondered if she could compete.

She should have been asking a different question. Was Jack even interested in giving her the chance?

Hot tears pricked her eyelids. She'd made a lot of mistakes, she knew that now, but this one hurt the most. And this one couldn't be corrected. She'd fallen in love with the wrong man.

* * *

Anita woke up determined to forget Jack Hayden. Unfortunately, when she walked into the nursery Sunday morning, the first thing she saw was the big, athletic male cradling a tiny baby. Jack's hand engulfed the baby's back, but his patting was *so* gentle.

She turned and fled.

Jack went after her, the baby still held at his shoulder. His legs were longer; he caught up. "Anita—wait. Let's talk."

"About what?" When he didn't answer right away, she went on, "I think you said more than enough last night!" She was shaking, *not* tingling in response to the melting allure of those great, toasty eyes.

"Come on, Anita. You know how confused I get. Please. I didn't mean everything I said last night. You know how much I care about you. We can work something out." He looked haggard—and sexy as hell with his tie loosened and the top button of his collar undone.

In self-defense, she tried to resist that megacharm and those vague promises. "You show your caring in very strange ways, Jack Hayden. Did you learn them in Hollywood or one of the other fifty places you've lived?"

"I guess you're saying you don't give points for effort around here." He looked sad. "It's no excuse, Anita, but... hotshot athletes... Well, I never had to work at a relationship before. I didn't have to be sincere or patient or concerned."

He shrugged. "I guess I don't do it very well." He gestured raggedly. "Look, Anita, once upon a time, I was young and successful and immortal. Then I became mortal—" He shrugged again. "I wasn't any more prepared for real life than anyone ever is."

Another shrug. The baby liked it; she gurgled. "But I'm trying! I picked myself up and learned humility, Anita. I learned perspective. I learned how to teach, too. I tried to learn how to fit in, how to help my friends the way people helped me."

A corner of Anita's mind thought she was so attuned to Jack Hayden that she knew what he meant without hearing the words plainly spoken. But another corner reminded her he hadn't mentioned marriage since getting that job offer.

"Anita, please." Jack interrupted her whirling thoughts. "Talk to me."

"About what?"

"Jesse. Marco. Indiana."

He started to add something but faltered into a silence broken only by baby gurgles.

Finally, Anita stopped waiting for what wasn't coming and broke the charged stillness. "I'd say there's nothing to talk about." She gazed at him, memorizing his troubled features. "You don't understand, do you?"

"Not completely."

"Then maybe you should just forget it."

Jack stared at her a long time, still patting the baby automatically. "It looks like you're giving me no choice, Ms. Valdez."

He and the baby went back to the nursery. Anita turned and went home. It was a strange, empty whimper of a goodbye.

Chapter Nine

Time passed with the dreamlike quality of a silent nightmare. While Jesse, who wasn't talking to her, played three more games for the Badgers—three victories of course—Anita sat numbly in the last row of the bleachers. She'd literally fled the field. The only way to get over Jack Hayden was to stay as far away from his tingle-force as possible.

And Jack cooperated. He ate lunch with his team now, only rarely looking in her direction, his face impassive. He attended church services in the sanctuary with everyone but Anita.

Her pillow was wet a few times when she woke up, but Anita wasn't crying over Jack Hayden. Not now, not ever. If he thought she ought to abandon her friends and family to grovel for the temporary affection of some overgrown, sexy, misguided, interfering, magnificent male with lost-puppy eyes and backward charm—he had another think coming.

When the news spread through town that he was taking Rita Pawelek to Irene and Joe's wedding, Anita didn't get upset. She got in her dumpy old vehicle that wasn't a hot red sports car and went shopping in the most exclusive San Antonio boutique she could find. She came home with a sinfully gorgeous yellow silk number that wiped out her Christmas fund but did fabulous things to her eyes, skin and figure; it was worth every penny. The whole of Larson probably expected her to stay home in some kind of self-imposed disgrace. They, too, had another think coming.

Anita hadn't done anything wrong—except fall in love with a man who thought Larson was too small, who said he came here looking for single women and who hadn't repeated his half-baked proposal once he had a sure ticket out of town.

All of which was no reason to miss her friends' wedding. She'd show Larson and Hollywood that she didn't care what Jack did with his social life.

She had to reapply her makeup three times that evening. Something in the air made tears roll down her cheeks and take her mascara along. Eventually, she gave the yellow silk a final pat, strapped on her highest heels and corralled her brother to be her escort, since surprisingly, he was still available.

Jesse was slow getting ready, which made them late to the church. When they finally arrived, there was only one place left to sit. Jesse hung back with surprising strength and she was forced to slide into the pew next to Jack. Rita smiled at her from his other side.

Anita missed the first half of the ceremony, lost in a longing she couldn't control. His cologne, his warmth, his closeness—her heart rebelled against her pride-filled head and called her an outright idiot for letting things end the way they did.

Well, what did she expect? Her silly heart still loved him.

Thanks to Jesse's perfect timing, Anita sat a heartbeat away. Jack surreptitiously tweaked a corner of the shirt the boy had helped him pick out. It was turquoise with a wide band of black, red and white Indian motifs across the chest and sleeves. It also had that funny curved western yoke.

The black jeans were normal, though wide enough through the lower leg to accommodate boots. He'd followed Jesse's advice to add a tooled belt and a bolo tie. Jack felt as self-conscious as a teenager.

He kept his eyes trained straight ahead and utilized his peripheral vision. Was she laughing at him behind that jet curtain of hair he wanted to slide his fingers through?

During the next musical interlude, Jack shifted in his seat. He needed to break the ice. *So say something, dope. But what? Better stick to something mundane.*

The wedding, he pointed out politely in a deep whisper, was a beautiful solemn ceremony, with a radiant bride and a beaming, nervous groom. Anita nodded but didn't reply.

"Perhaps you'll explain the white rope looped around their shoulders," he murmured to her as the nuptials concluded. "And the dimes in her shoe. I've never seen them before and Rita said she didn't know what they meant." It was only a tiny lie; he hadn't asked Rita.

Anita's cheeks colored. "They're Mexican traditions but everyone in Larson, including Rita Pawelek, knows them. Ask her again," she whispered back as the large wedding party streamed past. They were standing so close, but she was so far away!

"Are you considered Mexican, Anita?" When her head snapped around to aim lifted eyebrows at him, he backtracked, "Well, you're a Texan, for sure.... I suppose your wedding will feature these rites, too?"

"My marriage will be celebrated very much like this—in typical Larson fashion," she replied stiffly.

He started to say something, but changed it. Safety first. At least she was talking to him. "This seems like a normal wedding to me."

"You haven't seen the reception, Hollywood. Define normal after you survive that."

Jack caught himself cocking his hip and throwing back his shoulders in one of those old macho-hotshot poses. As he called himself down, Jesse whispered in his ear, "She's been crying again, but she's still ticked off. Big-time."

Jesse's warning and the odd glow in Anita's eyes that he couldn't interpret worried Jack, but the way she kept glancing at him... Jack decided the western outfit was worth every penny he'd spent. "Thanks for your help, son. If things work out, I may be your relative as well as your coach."

Jack hardly felt the teen's bashful punch on his arm; his body still burned from the accidental touch of Anita's arm as she'd brushed past him a minute ago.

Luckily, Rita jangled her bracelets at him before the hope that sang in his veins made him do something stupid.

"Come on, Rita. Let's go to this reception deal." He touched Jesse's arm. "She coming?"

"Yeah, Coach." Jesse's voice dropped to a conspiratorial whisper. "I did like you suggested and challenged her pride. She'll be there." The boy trotted away.

"Sorry, Rita. I don't mean to be rude—" He'd recruited the woman with full disclosure: he wanted one last chance to make Anita see sense, and he thought a wedding might be a romantic enough occasion to weaken her resistance.

Rita grinned at him. "Hey, I've got the picture," she assured him, "but you'd better make your move soon. She isn't going to stand for much more."

"*She* isn't—! Look, Rita, I haven't done anything wrong. She's the one who needs to get her head straight."

"Do you love her?" Rita had her hands on her hips. They were no doubt very sexy hips, but Jack didn't notice or care.

"Hell, yes. What's that got to do with it?"

"Love has everything to do with it. It's the only thing, actually, that matters."

"Tell *her* that," Jack suggested glumly, escorting Rita to his sports car.

"No, you tell her," Rita insisted. "Then tell her again. Tell her till she hears you. Make her believe it."

Jack followed the rest of the witnesses down the road leading out of Larson. "Where are we going?" he asked as the town faded into the dark behind them.

"They rented the parish hall at Panna Maria," Rita explained. "It's about ten minutes from Larson. If you can persuade Anita to marry you, the whole town will expect to be invited, you know. Panna Maria ought to be just about big enough for your reception. You'll see."

She was right: he saw. And Anita was right about the reception: it was something to be survived. Jack was surprised they didn't sell T-shirts declaring that message. Perhaps one hundred fifty people had attended the church ceremony; the reception involved about four times that number. Sequestering Anita until he figured out what to say and she listened to it was going to be a tough play.

The "hall," which he'd pictured as a church-basement sort of setting, *was* Panna Maria. The rest of the town consisted of the large, beautiful church that owned the hall, a small store post office, and about three houses. The hall—actually three or four separate wooden buildings, connected by roofed walkways—took up two city-size blocks. The main building was a huge rectangle with slatted covers over the windows, hinged at the top like trapdoors. As they followed the string of cars past it, someone was propping open the coverings. Billows of smoke from the far corner of the compound indicated the barbecue area. It had two pits the size of small pickup trucks for cooking or smoking; Rita said the bride's family had begun preparing the meat before dawn.

After parking in an adjacent grassy field, they walked back toward the hall. Through the crisp night air, he could hear a band warming up in the main building. Above them, a double handful of stars twinkled in the huge dark sky. Slow, twangy greetings floated around them.

"There she is," Rita said, pointing. "And there's my brother Dale. I'm going to see my new nephew, so you go over to Anita and get to work."

"Thanks, Rita."

"Thank me later. Now go."

"You ladies look exquisite this evening," he said, sliding up behind them. "Your dress is very becoming, Anita. Yours too, Leticia," he told the youngest Valdez. "Your ruffles are spectacular."

Letty beamed with pleasure. And Anita had jumped a foot at his greeting. So far, so good. He still affected her senses—he'd exploit that one weakness in her defenses until he found a way to get back in the game.

"You...look nice, too...Jack." Anita's response sounded like an electronic message.

Darn it, he couldn't even figure out what he'd done wrong! How could he repair something he didn't even understand? He didn't want to go to Indiana, but if Anita needed an added inducement to take him on, he'd call Dub tonight.

On the other hand, if he could convince her that quality of life in Larson outweighed plain money... Jack sighed. He was getting ahead of himself.

And he was stumped for a next step to take. Uncertain, afraid he'd make the wrong move and never get another chance. Was he going to lose the one time he wanted desperately to win? He stuck to nonsense for now.

"That's all you can say?" He kept his voice light and amused. He deserved an Academy Award for this performance! "Jesse told me this was an 'awesome' shirt. I'm pretty sure that's a lot more than nice."

"I think you look very, very handsome, Mr. Coach Jack," Leticia said solemnly.

"Thanks, sweetie," Jack flashed the little girl a smile. "Will you save me a dance later?"

Letty giggled. "Sure, Mr. Coach!"

When Anita still didn't say anything, Jack thrust an imaginary microphone at her. "And what's your *real* opinion of the outfit, Nurse Valdez?"

At last, she looked at him. The corners of her mouth turned minutely, delightfully upward. "You know you look as hot as high noon in July, so why ask? Rita'll be all over you tonight like flies on—"

"Anita!" Jack cut her off, jerking his chin downward. "Little pitchers—"

"Are not immune to your charm, either, Mr. Coach Jack," Anita said, nodding her permission when Letty wanted to join some friends.

Jack racked his brain for some way to keep a conversation going. "I know more people here tonight than I did at my sister's wedding."

No answer. He plowed on. "So you think the clothes are okay? That I blend into the crowd?" He threw her a significant look, but Anita dodged it.

"I'm sure Rita's impressed with your attempt to fit in."

"Rita's only a friend, Anita. You know that. I had to see you again." Jack tried to caress her with his smile, but it was probably too dark for her to see it.

"No doubt this reception will be dull by your standards."

He felt a touch of panic at the coolness of her tone and retreated to generalities. "Somehow, five or six hundred Texans intent on having a good time doesn't sound dull at all."

It wasn't. Like everything else, they seemed to do weddings bigger in Texas. Six hundred people consumed their fill of barbecued beef, beans, potato salad, bread, pickles and onions, washed down with gallons of beer from kegs set up in a row like the heads on Easter Island; barrels of tea and washtubs filled with iced-down sodas eased the thirst of nonimbibers. As soon as the bride and groom pushed pieces of cake into each other's faces, everyone else stormed the cake tables.

Throughout the ordeal, Jack tried to maneuver himself close to Anita but she kept slipping away. Just like his chance for happiness and he didn't understand what was going wrong. He'd made amends for his past, hadn't he?

Dammit, he was a nice guy now—did that mean he was doomed to finish last?

Well, the game wasn't over until she married somebody else. And he had a few more moves to try. He headed off to find his "date."

When the dance got under way, Jack and Rita played a little scene in front of Anita that didn't fool the floorboards.

Ms. Pawelek had a headache and needed a few hours to find some aspirin. Jack wanted to dance. Well, maybe somebody else could dance with him. Like synchronized robots, they turned and looked at Anita.

Who did they think they were fooling? Anita wondered as she gazed back at them, unconsciously lifting her chin.

In spite of their initial differences and her wounded pride at his interference with the way she handled her brother and her embarrassment at falling for his marriage line, Jack still made her feel crazy inside, like thunder and lightning, a willing and weak-kneed fool. But that didn't change a thing. He was too big for Larson and Larson was her home. She had no intention of making things harder for herself.

But when Rita left and Jack asked Anita to dance, she nodded. So much for philosophy and principles. Silly heart wanted one last moment with him, a memory to hold on to when he was gone.

They watched the bride and groom take the floor to start the dance. "I'm wearing the proper footwear tonight," Jack said, indicating his flat-soled ropers. "But I'm better at the waltz." Irene and Joe Janek were two-stepping to their favorite song.

"You're a Yankee," Anita replied, trying to remember that Jack's rejection made their love affair a dead issue. "Nobody expects you to know how to western-dance."

"Oh, but I do, Ms. Valdez." Despite his laconic delivery, his pride was obvious. "I've been taking private lessons."

The air suddenly turned to ice. Had a norther blown in? "Private lessons?" Anita echoed against her will. Had Jack actually lied to her? She'd never thought he could. Her heart sank. So there *was* something between him and Rita, after all.

"Yeah." Jack's grin turned the ice to steam. Oh, damn him! "Mrs. Floyd's been tutoring me while I do my laundry."

Mrs. Floyd was the seventy-year-old owner of the laundromat. "You do it deliberately, don't you?" Anita asked as the bride began dancing with her father, the groom with his mother.

"Yes, ma'am," he admitted with that irresistible grin. "It's the only sign of encouragement I get—those little hackles that rise when you think I might be interested in another woman."

With a hand on her back, Jack guided her onto the dance floor when the rest of the crowd surged forward. "I know you're mad at me for what happened at the Homecoming dance," he said as he carefully guided Anita around the hall in time with the music. "What else have I done wrong? Oh, yes—I've tried to help with your brother's college expenses."

Anita did an underarm turn. "By prolonging his involvement with a dangerous contact sport."

"I guess that's an apt description," he said gravely. "Except that it's no more dangerous than anything else in life. It's just the one thing, for some reason, you think you should control."

That odd something flashed in her eyes. "There's no point in discussing this again, Jack. You have your opinion. I have mine. And it won't matter soon, anyway."

"I don't know what you mean, Anita. Why won't it matter? Jesse will always be your brother, just like I'll always—" Jack clamped his mouth shut. The only things he could think of to say would either commit him to leaving Larson or make him sound like a lovesick idiot. Or both.

And he had a little pride left. Despite Rita's advice, he couldn't tell Anita he loved her again until he saw some real sign of encouragement. And he wasn't going to leave Larson, Texas, unless she forced him to.

"I'll always be willing to help kids like Jesse and Marco," he finished lamely.

Anita stopped dead on the dance floor.

"Well, congratulations, Mr. Hayden. The big hero who solves everyone's problems." She stormed off.

"Except my own," Jack muttered, stuck in the middle of a two-stepping mob.

Vern and his wife whirled past. "Don't worry, Jack. She'll come around if Jesse gets that scholarship."

Jack shook his head and walked to the edge of the crowd. The boys had received official scholarship offers, but it wasn't common knowledge because Anita wouldn't even look at the papers and Danny's parents said he couldn't go without Jesse.

Jack had counseled patience, but Jesse had blown up, tired of waiting. Part of the purpose of tonight's plot had been to reconcile brother and sister. *Another brilliant tactical screwup, Hayden!* Would he ever learn?

"Hi, Anita. You and Jack get things straightened out?" Rita blocked the foot of the dance-hall porch. The fringe and rhinestones on her fitted blouse accented the curves of her spectacular figure.

"No. I'm going to help in the kitchen," Anita said evenly. "You enjoy yourself with the coach, Rita." As she started to push past the other woman, she felt a hand on her arm.

"Don't forfeit the game to someone who isn't even on the field, okay?"

"I don't know what you're talking about."

Rita shrugged and released her. "Then you're a bigger fool than I thought."

When Anita returned from dishwashing duty half an hour later, the band was announcing the dollar dance. She hadn't been inside the building thirty seconds when Jack appeared. "What are they doing now?" he asked, his hand circling her waist as if it belonged there. As if she hadn't left him stranded on the dance floor.

Which one of us is crazier? Anita wondered. She was leaning into him, like a shivering kitten seeking warmth.

Rita was across the room, arm in arm with the gunsmith from Kenedy.

"It's a custom around here," Anita explained, twisting out of his embrace even as she longed to stay within it. "The single guys take turns. They pay the bride a dollar to dance with her until another guy gives her a dollar to cut in. It's a way to raise money for a honeymoon."

Jack barely glanced at the action on the dance floor, though he dug a bill out of his pocket. "Anita, let's try one more—"

Her heart was racing with the heat in his eyes, but her head remembered her internal dishwashing lectures. "It's another quaint Larson tradition you can amuse people with next year." She arranged the dollar in his hand properly. "Go out there and dance."

Anita pushed him onto the floor. She didn't tell him it was also a tradition to make a newcomer dance forever before the next man rescued him. The crowd got a good laugh when the band switched to a polka as soon as Jack took up his position with the bride. Irene led him through a series of advanced versions of the pretzel turns.

Despite her absolute intention to cultivate disinterest in Jack Hayden, Anita couldn't help being proud of his reaction to the trickery. Jack laughed and played along, pretending to desperately seek rescue as Irene tangled him in the complex turns. How many men would happily allow themselves to be public spectacles? That was why she loved him: even played for a fool, he looked perfectly at home, perfectly human, perfectly happy.

When Jack was finally replaced by another dancer, he walked off the floor to a round of shouted cheers and applause. He raised his hands in a victory salute, looked at Rita, then headed straight for Anita. She turned and hit the exit at a dead run, seeking her only true refuge from another assault by the sensual power of Jack Hayden: the women's rest room.

Her defenses were useless against him. No matter how much she loved her brother and wanted to protect him, no matter how much she wanted to stay near her parents' memory, no matter how much she wanted to remain the source of medical care for Larson County, she loved Jack Hayden. She couldn't stop it. Couldn't get over it. Ever.

But she couldn't marry him, couldn't move from town to town for his job. She needed roots. She wouldn't ask him to change; she couldn't beg him to stay. She understood that he was trying to be kind in his own way. He hadn't repeated his proposal, hadn't mentioned that job in Indiana because he knew she wanted to stay in Larson and he intended to leave. He didn't want to make her choose.

And still, she wanted him. It was impossible!

Anita pressed a moistened paper towel against her eyes. A noise startled her and she lowered the rough, wet blindfold.

Someone was clearing her throat. It was Rita Pawelek. Probably wanted to touch up her hair or—*grrr*—even worse, her lipstick for Jack.

Anita moved away from the tiny mirror.

"Anita, I didn't mean to get caught in the middle."

The situation wasn't Rita's fault. It wasn't even Jack's. It was Anita's. She'd given her heart to the only man who made her tremble. And he'd politely given it back.

Anita smoothed her skirt. "It's okay, Rita. Did you want something?" *Besides Jack Hayden.*

Rita cleared her throat again. "Jack only asked me to come with him tonight so he could talk to you. You're a fool to stay mad at him."

"Maybe I *don't* want to talk to you, Rita," Anita said slowly.

Rita flushed. "Come on, 'Nita. Lighten up. Jack's trying to tell you something any woman in her right mind wants to hear. You know how Jack is—he goes off half-cocked, but he means well. Why don't you give him a break?"

Before Anita could respond, Rita changed the subject. "Actually, I didn't come in here to discuss your personal life. I came to ask for a ride home."

That left Anita totally bewildered. "Why don't you go home with Jack? No! I mean, why doesn't Jack take you home?"

A corner of Rita's mouth quirked up. "I'd love to go home with Jack, but he's not even remotely interested in anyone not named Valdez."

Maybe Jesse Valdez.

Rita went on with a shake of fringe, "He asked me a few minutes ago to find a ride home. Dale and Ed left earlier and I can't find Danny or Dad."

"Okay, Rita, let me know when you're ready."

"I'm ready any time you are."

"Let's go find Jesse." It would be a relief to escape further encounters with Jack Hayden.

Jesse was with Jack in the middle of a group of exuberant young males. When Anita drew her brother aside, he refused to leave.

"Tío Juan said it was okay. I'll be home later." Should she argue with him over this, too? His face was in shadow, but his feelings about her interference were clear enough.

Anita suddenly understood. Jesse wasn't rebelling against her. He was simply making the transition from child to man. Trying to hold him back was fighting a losing battle—and the only loser would be her.

Reaching over to ruffle his hair, Anita surrendered. "I'm sorry, Jesse. I guess—I've been trying to hold on to Papa and Mama by holding on to you. I'll learn to let go."

Jesse remained still, but his muscles relaxed. Finally, he said, "You'll still be my sister, won't you?"

"You bet."

After a fierce hug, Jesse cleared his throat. "Sis—"

"Go on back to your friends, Jesse, and have fun, but—be careful."

She could hear the grin in his voice. "No sweat. Studied with an expert."

It was almost three in the morning when Jesse got home. In Jack's car. As he walked past Anita, who'd fallen asleep on the couch, he mumbled, "I'll return it later. He said s'okay."

When Jack didn't show up at church in the morning, Anita decided that even if she wasn't talking to him, a few things needed to be explained.

"Jesse, give me Jack's keys," she demanded when she got home from nursery duty. There was something roiling through her insides. She didn't know exactly what it was, but she knew its source: Jack "Hollywood" Hayden.

Jesse rubbed his eyes and pointed to the dresser. "Should I follow you over there and give you a ride home?" He looked at his sister. "Never mind. Dumb question. You need a ride, call me at Danny's."

Anita picked up the keys and turned toward the door. "What exactly were you guys doing last night?"

Jesse manufactured a superb unjustly accused tone. "I wasn't doing anything. The older guys were doing shots."

That explains it, Anita thought as she drove to Jack's apartment. Explains why he let Jesse drop him off. And why he missed church: he's hung over or sleeping it off. Or both.

She knocked sharply on his door, turned the knob and opened it.

"Come on back." The instruction came from the bedroom.

Jack getting drunk, especially in public, didn't feel right, but there was no denying his voice was tight with pain.

Anita stopped in the bedroom doorway. Jack was sitting on the edge of a rumpled bed, a wad of sheet covering his lap. For a second, the sight of his magnificent form banished all thoughts of detective work. His smooth golden-skinned chest was lightly covered with crinkly hair, his muscles promised power and pleasure.

Waves of longing pulled her into the room like a magnetic force. She imagined caressing his warm skin, being drawn down into those tangled sheets, pressed against the mattress by his weight, his hands stroking, his lips lingering....

Jack's lips were pressed together in a thin white line, his eyes squeezed shut. His hair was a mess of delightful little peaks, she noted absently, already on her way across the tiny bedroom to his side.

Because Jack's hands weren't holding his aching head. They were clasped around his left, very scarred knee. The one that was at least twice normal size.

Then Anita was kneeling beside the bed, gently smoothing her hands over the joint, making a swift professional exploration. "My God, Jack, what happened?"

His voice was raspy with the effort to contain the pain. "Irene and Joe got married."

"What?"

"I'm sorry, Anita. I thought you knew."

"Knew what?"

Jack's hand circled the swollen knee. "About my knee. It's the reason I left professional football. It's how I knew what the risks are and what Marco felt. Everything."

"You also knew this would happen if you went to the reception and danced." The statement barely skirted being a question.

"It was the biggest event in Larson this month. And you were going to be there. I wanted to see you, talk to you." Jack looked at her with an intensity that sent those familiar tingles through her like high-voltage bursts. "I wouldn't have missed that wedding for the world."

"But your knee—" Her hands shook a little as she cradled it gently.

"—pays a price. Small one for the privilege of dancing with you."

"I saw you limping sometimes, knew you'd retired early, but—I didn't know your injury was that bad," she said softly, raising her eyes to his face.

"Actually, the repair job was that good. I wasn't supposed to be able to walk on it again." Jack's hands gripped the edge of the bed dislodging the sheet. When her eyes slid downward and widened, he—slowly—readjusted his cover and managed to turn one corner of his mouth upward. "Only the knee's damaged," he assured her with a trace of male smugness. "The rest of me works fine."

"I'll get some ice for your knee," Anita said and fled.

Jack had time to pull on sweatpants and a T-shirt before she returned. With obviously practiced moves, he hobbled into the living room, fell into the sagging armchair there, propped his leg on the matching ancient footstool and applied the ice pack expertly to his knee. Then he indicated the sofa. "Please—sit down. Forgive my manners."

Anita waved away his apology with a small, brief frown. "You knew dancing would aggravate it."

"Geez, Anita, you make it sound like I committed a crime. I didn't know dancing on a bum knee was a felony." He was trying to joke, but his voice was still strained. Anita got up and went into his bathroom. She returned with two small white tablets and a glass of water.

"Take them," she said, indicating the pills.

"Yes, ma'am." He followed instructions. "Thank you."

After a few moments of silence, Anita crossed her legs, sat back on the sofa and asked quietly, "Was that—" she gestured at his knee "—why Jesse brought you home?"

Jack shook his head. "No. Those groomsmen were doing shots." Anita nodded and Jack continued, "Apparently, it's another common wedding custom around here like the dollar dance. A dollar buys a shot of whiskey, with the buyer having the option of drinking it himself or making the best man toss it back."

She nodded again, a little impatiently. Why was Jack explaining local customs to her?

"Anita, these young guys think they're immortal. They were planning on driving themselves and their dates home."

She bit her lip. "I know. It's a problem, but it's one of those traditions that are hard to break."

Jack didn't seem to hear her. "It wasn't my place to interfere, but after all our discussions about risk-taking... Well, I know firsthand that the unthinkable can happen. I sure as hell never planned on my knee being destroyed on the first play of my second season, ending my career at the beginning...." He shrugged off the details.

"Anyway, I thought if I had a little influence, I ought to use it. So I collected car keys and arranged for Jesse and some of the boys old enough to drive and too young to drink—with their coach around, anyway—to be a taxi service. I let Jesse use my car to follow the taxi drivers to their destinations and take them back to Panna Maria to pick up their own vehicles."

She came across the room and her arms circled his neck. He knew his pulse speeded up with her touch. He didn't try to control the response; he tried to enjoy it, because it might be the last time she touched him. Basically, she knew all the bad stuff now: big mouth, bad knee, no taste for fast living. And of course, she still hadn't forgiven him for his other sins, whatever they were exactly.

"You make me so mad sometimes, Jack, the way you treat this town like you invented it, but this time—thank you," she whispered and hugged him tight.

Don't let go, he begged silently, but said nothing aloud.

As though she could read his mind, she released him. She sat back on the sofa and said, "Jack, I want... I wish..." Her eyes fell to his waist, dropped farther, then veered toward the bedroom.

Jack hoped his heart would stay inside his chest.

He sat rigidly in the armchair wrestling with his libido, while Anita hid behind a swinging curtain of hair. He wanted her—had wanted her since the first moment he saw her. He knew he could make her happy, knew he'd do everything in his power to make her happy—in bed and out—for a lifetime.

Who cares about unresolved difficulties? I love her, he argued with himself. *I love her enough for both of us. And if I could be with her once... at least I'll have one memory of satisfying the woman I love. Maybe it won't be enough, but it would be something. And maybe it would convince her of my love, since I can't seem to put it into words right.*

Jack looked at Anita. Her hands were clasped white-knuckled, her knees were pressed tightly together. Obviously, she'd remembered why she was mad at him. Would she ever tell him where he'd gone wrong?

He ought to ask, but somehow, hearing her put it into words would make it irrefutably real. Like carving it in stone.

"I'll take you home," he said and began unwrapping the ice pack.

"No need. I called Jesse while you were dressing and he's picking me up." She looked at the clock. "In about five minutes."

Jack started to tease her about awkward explanations to brothers, but a synapse in his brain finally closed and made a new connection. He suddenly translated her body language correctly. "You...you never—"

"It's none of your business and what difference would it make?" Her chin lifted defiantly. "It just means that Larson's a small town and I'm a small-town girl."

Jack spread his hands out, palms up. "It means," he corrected her gently, "that waiting is important to you." He was silent, then— "God, Anita, what kind of man do you think I am?"

His eyes became green ice. "You think I'd use pity to manipulate people for selfish reasons?"

"Jack, I'm sorry about your knee."

"Well, I'm not. I sure as hell don't sit around feeling sorry for myself. I suppose I could. After all, I could be making millions of dollars now playing professional football, but that's not the way things worked out and I'm grateful."

"Oh, right. You expect me to believe this is your ideal." Her sweeping hand included the tiny apartment, small school, Larson itself.

His deep voice, rich with conviction, overrode her incredulity. "It could have been. Look, Anita, it's all luck or fate or something. If this knee hadn't been crushed and my football career ended so early, I wouldn't have come to Larson, wouldn't have been able to help some kids who could use a little assistance. And I wouldn't have met you, so I would have never known what love is."

"Jack, I—"

"Or how much love hurts," he added softly and struggled to his feet. "I think it was worth it, but I also think you'd better go, Anita."

"But I—"

"I have no regrets. I love you, but I can only promise you myself. I can't give you guarantees of financial security or safety or success. It wouldn't be right—and neither of us would end up happy. See, Anita, that's the real thing we disagree about. Life. You have to take it as it comes, however much it hurts, or you never live at all."

Anita was struck dumb. While she struggled to sort out the implications of his speech, a familiar horn honked. "That's Jesse," she said, jumping up.

Holding the front door open, she paused. "Are you going to be here later?"

Jack was replacing the ice pack around his knee. "I'm not going anywhere," he assured her.

Was there another meaning deep in his crystal-clear eyes? She wanted so much to believe it, but... Could she survive the disillusionment if she was wrong?

Anita turned and left the apartment. In the car, she directed Jesse to make a slight detour. "We need to go by Ira Smolik's."

Forty minutes later, she walked back into Jack's apartment and handed him a milk-white bottle with a handwritten label: *Liniment, half-strength.* "Rub that on your knee every four hours," she said and looked at him.

It was time to be completely honest.

"Jesse told me about your job offer in Indiana," she said softly as tears gathered in her eyes. "I'm glad for you—I know you need new challenges. It's just as well you didn't repeat that marriage proposal, because I want to stay here in Larson where I belong. Where I'm needed. I know you cared for me...."

Silently, Jack stared at her with those big golden-green eyes that she'd see forever.

She forced herself to go on. "But I understand. Now that your coaching career's taking off, you want to keep your options open."

Jack made an inarticulate noise in the back of his throat. Anita held up her hand. "Don't say anything. I know you'll try to be kind and... I was wrong. You're a nice man, Jack. Not Hollywood Hayden, after all."

She bent and kissed his cheek, then straightened up. "I don't think we should see each other again, Jack, except across the cafeteria." A little sob escaped her lips. "I couldn't bear it."

Before he could say anything, she left again, tears trickling down her cheeks.

Chapter Ten

‘Look, Sis, you’ve got to snap out of this.’’ Jesse stood
ver the chair in which Anita slumped. ‘‘You’ve been
alking around like a zombie for a week. Come look at the
ess in my room—yell at me. It’ll make you feel better.’’
When Anita didn’t respond, Jesse’s face clouded up.
Darn it, Sis—it’s your own fault, you know.’’
She looked at him dully.
‘‘You could have had it all, Sis,’’ Jesse said, his frown
epening, ‘‘but for some crazy reason, you threw it away.
nd now all you do is mope around. What the heck’s
rong with you?’’
Instead of shouting back, Anita’s eyes filled with tears
d she covered her face with her hands. ‘‘I’ve messed
erything up, haven’t I? Not just for me.... Oh, Jesse, I’m
rry. I didn’t want to let go of Mama and Papa—I guess I
ought if I acted like them, they’d sort of...still be here.’’
e tears trickled down her cheeks.
Jesse patted her shoulder awkwardly.
‘‘You’re right, you know. I’m a lousy parent. I don’t
ow what I’m doing. You go to Indiana and study engi-

eering. I'll sign the papers. I'll quit bird-dogging you. A
soon as Jack leaves, I'll—"

"You'll what?"

"Well, I don't know. It doesn't matter." Anita shook h
head sadly and wiped at the moisture in her eyes.

Jesse sank to his knees beside her chair. "Please, 'Nit
Don't. I'm sorry. Forget Indiana, just... Please, pleas
don't be disappointed in me," he begged.

Anita looked up at the broken sound of her brother
voice.

"I couldn't stand it if you... if something happened
you and it was my fault, too."

Somewhere inside her own pain, Anita recognized th
oblique reference to whatever had been bothering h
brother all these months. She recognized a cry for hel
Maybe she was parent material, after all. "What do yo
mean—your fault, *too?*" she asked gently.

The words came out haltingly at first, then in a floo
mingled with choking sobs. "Mama and Papa—th
night... the night of the fire—we had an argument abo
me going out too much instead of studying. I l-left. To
Papa I wasn't coming home and he just gave me that sa
look of his." Anita remembered the look—it had been ve
effective on her, too. "I spent the night at Danny's. Don
you see, 'Nita? If I hadn't stomped out, our paren
wouldn't be dead! It's my fault!"

Five hundred pounds of tension instantly lifted off An
ta's shoulders. "Oh, Jesse, no! That's not true! Why, yo
might have died, too." She pulled him into her arms and f
once he let her. "Jesse, what happened was a tragic acc
dent but it wasn't your fault. It was an old house—the wi
ing was bad. There wasn't anything you could have done
change what happened.

"It was just an accident," she repeated. "We have
accept it and go on. We can't change the past. You can't l
it ruin the rest of your life. The important thing is to lo
each other, cherish each other while we have the chance.
be a family, together, as long as we're alive. The rest-

ootball, college, grades—doesn't matter. It's just windo
dressing."

After a long silence, Jesse grinned shakily. "Did you hear what you just said, Sis? It might apply to you, too."

Anita cocked her head to one side, then weakly grinned back. "Okay, smarty-pants. Once in a while, teenagers are ight—but it's only blind luck!"

Jesse scrambled to his feet, already recovered enough to e embarrassed by his emotional outburst. "So what are ou going to do about it? You gonna call the coach nd...er, whatever?"

Ask him straight out if he still wants to marry me?

Anita considered the idea, then shook her head regret-ully. "I think it's going to take more than an apologetic hone call to fix this."

"But he's crazy about you."

"Was, maybe. Now..." Anita shook her head and smiled vistfully. "Look, Jesse, I love Larson, I'd like to stay here orever. But the bottom line is that Jack—your coach is oing to Indiana. And he hasn't asked me to go with him."

She stood up. Some things couldn't be mended, but some ould. "Anyway, little brother, it's my problem. I'll deal vith it. As for you, young man, you'd better get that room leaned up and crack open those books—engineers can't be aught unprepared. I'll find you some food to put in that ver-empty stomach."

She squeezed Jesse's biceps playfully. "Winning playoff ames takes energy, too, kid!"

Jack worked overtime to run into Anita because he vasn't going to actively pursue her anymore. A man had a ertain amount of pride, after all. If she wanted to jump to liotic conclusions about him, maybe he should rethink his eelings for her. *Rethink his feelings? Oh, good, Jack, you an't even make sense to yourself!*

After almost a week of trying unsuccessfully to encoun-er her casually, he turned to the next best source. "Say, esse. What's that stuff your sister gave me for my knee?"

'It's horse liniment, Coach."

"You're kidding."

Jesse shook his head, chuckling. "Nope. Ira Smolik makes it up for his horses."

"Hmm—that does explain the tremendous urge I have t jump fences on the way to school."

Jesse's laugh reminded Jack of Anita's. *That sound wa worth the world,* Jack thought, while he berated himself fo his idiotic lapse into nobility after that wedding. Principle be hanged—he should have heard that laughter in his bed Instead, he might never hear it again.

He knew in his heart his noble decision had been th correct one: he didn't want to visit heaven with Anita fo fifteen minutes; he wanted a lifetime with his angel "Where's your sister?" Jack demanded, then backed off "I mean, I haven't seen her around lately."

Jesse ignored the question. "Everybody in the count uses the liniment. Sis says it's no cure, but it reduces th swelling and pain."

"You're right—my knee feels almost normal."

"Look, Coach—I gotta go. 'Nita's around." The bo gestured vaguely, then shifted his weight from foot to foo while he pondered a decision of some kind. Finally, Jess said, "Look, Coach, some people like small towns, som like big cities."

Jack pinned him with a look. "Talk straight, Jesse, o you're riding the bench."

"'Nita thinks you don't want her 'cuz you're taking tha job in Indiana. 'Sides, she wants to stay here," the bo blurted out, then flashed a grin at Jack's stunned look "But I think her mind could be changed. For some rea son, she's more stuck on you than on Larson. Well, bye Coach, gotta go!" Jesse escaped between clumps of gig gling girls.

Jack was stranded in the cafeteria, muttering unsports manlike imprecations under his breath. Then he started frantic search. Anita wasn't around Larson High. Sh wasn't anywhere he could find her. Nobody could tell hi where she'd gone or when she'd be back. Jack was so distraught, he held the practices to prepare for the next playoff round, but they didn't hold one iota of his attention. That was owned solely, completely, absolutely by the too-missing Ms. Valdez.

The regional playoff game was held at a neutral site an hour from Larson. Jack knew that keeping the boys calm before the game was important. If he could distract them long enough to get their jitters under control, they'd be fine. So now he stood, swaying with the vehicle, facing the rear of the bus, shooting the breeze with the most highly strung players.

During a lull in his part of the conversation, an insightful discussion of—what else?—teenage girls, Jack looked out the vehicle's back window. At that moment, the bus was topping a small rise and he saw a seemingly endless string of cars trailing behind them to the horizon.

The solid display of support pleased him. "You know, if anybody wanted to steal anything in Larson, now would be the time to do it," he joked, indicating the parade behind them. "It looks like the whole town's coming to watch us."

The sudden silence told him he'd done it again. "And they damn well should," he declared in a rush. "Because we're going to crush those wimps from Boyletown. Hell, the game'll be over in the first five minutes. Why, we're gonna kick the sh—"

"Coach, don't you think you'd better watch your mouth?" The sharp reminder came from one of the worst former offenders, now fervently reformed. Jack grinned at him weakly and took a deep breath. "Yeah, son, thanks. I guess I still get carried away sometimes."

Somebody snickered. "I'll say you do, Coach!" Danny chortled as he elbowed a grinning Bubba. "Remember when we saw the coach and Jesse's sister getting carried away along the Poth road."

And Lord, if he didn't feel himself blush! "We went to dinner in Floresville," he insisted, even as he wondered why

was defending his exemplary behavior to a bunch o
igh-school boys. *Because he fervently wished it hadn'*
been!

He'd had enough of this emptiness, this loneliness. If i
was a question of a coaching job or Anita, there was n
question. He'd sell peanut butter to cows. Didn't Anit
know she was more important to his life than anything else
He'd stay in Larson or fly to the moon, whatever sh
wanted. If he could only find her to tell her so! Oh, the hec
with words—they were part of the problem. He was goin
to have to show her.

"We stopped to study the sky—there was a rare con
junction of planets visible that night."

The whole bus hooted and guffawed. "Yeah, Coach, I'l
bet," Danny said, then looked around. "Anybody bring
pencil—we gotta write that one down!'

Well, at least they forgot to be nervous!

When the bus arrived at the playoff site and disgorge
the Fighting Badgers, Anita was at a pay phone in Indi
ana, trying to call Danny Pawelek's mother. By the tim
she'd boarded a plane for St. Louis, Dallas and San Anto
nio, the Badgers were surrounded by cheering fans, al
ready looking forward to their first championship game i
twenty years.

On to State read the signs in all the store windows o
Main Street as Anita cruised slowly through town, lookin
for Jack's red car. She'd been gone almost a week, swear
ing Jesse to secrecy and then not telling him anything h
could blab.

Anita looked at Larson through new eyes. She'd alway
thought it was a little town where nothing much changed.

Now, she knew better. In a week, whole lives ha
changed. From the exhortations of the signs, it appeare
whole fortunes were changing. No team from Larson ha
ever had a winning season in living memory. Now, the
were aiming at a state championship.

Anita gave up her hunt for the red sports car. She kn
where it and its owner would be Monday. She'd better sta
working on her speech—the one in which she explained
everything eloquently enough to convince Jack to give her a second chance. The one that made him want to repeat that marriage-license offer. The one she intended to make right after she kissed the fool out of him, handed him Dub's formal job offer and showed him the sheaf of job applications and apartment-rental brochures she'd gathered during her week in Indiana.

Fate refused to cooperate with Anita's speech-making plan. From the moment she returned to Larson, she was inundated. Emergency calls hit an all-time high for frequency and duration. Babies insisted on making their appearance, scheduled or not. State and county officials kept any remaining hours occupied with urgent paperwork demands. Or Jack was trapped on the practice field or in class.

The timing was never right, but she wasn't going to give her speech in public! It—and Jack's answer—would be all over town soon enough, anyway.

By the time the Reynoldses' baby arrived on Saturday afternoon, Larson was deserted and Anita realized she'd forgotten to ask Jesse where they were playing this week.

She also realized she couldn't stay away from Jack Hayden one more minute. Game or no game, babies or funding deadlines, Anita was going to find Jack and talk him into giving her one more chance. Now.

She called the sports department of the San Antonio newspaper.

"*Express-News*. Sports." The voice was as flat as a sheet of plywood.

"Er, could you tell me where the Larson Badgers are playing today? It's the Class 1A playoffs. In football," she added, trying to be helpful.

"Really? I thought you meant washer-pitching," the voice suggested snidely. "The Badgers are playing this afnoon at . . ." There was a pause to rustle papers. "Two p.m. at Alamo Stadium. Across from Trinity University."

"Thank you."

The voice actually sounded human at last. "Don't mention it. You a Badgers fan? Wasn't that bidistrict game incredible? Larson comes from behind and scores twice in the last two minutes! Man, that kind of cliffhanger went out with Staubach and the Cowboys. The Larson coach is some kind of genius! He called a double dogleg Z option . . ."

Since the voice had stopped speaking English—and, more importantly, had told her what she needed to know, Anita hung up gently.

Then she set a speed record from Larson to San Antonio.

The parking lot in front of the stadium was far from full, but the small clot of people milling around the ticket windows looked disgruntled. At another time, Anita might have paused, then advanced more slowly, drawing discouraging conclusions from the behavior of the crowd.

This time, however, as she'd pulled her car into a parking space, she'd seen a yellow school bus with a familiar rust spot beneath the right rear brake light and she knew who had ridden it from Larson. And she knew she couldn't stand to be so close and so far from him for more than about five minutes longer.

She strode across the concrete to the ticket window with a smile and the confidence of conviction. Anita was on her way to take the biggest risk of her life. She intended to dive headfirst into adventure, the unknown, and yes, danger, too, by giving her heart to the man it had been made for: a traveling football coach, a man with warm hazel eyes, a tangled tongue and a big kind heart. He simply couldn't kiss her like that and then change his mind.

"I'd like a ticket to the Larson-whoever game, please," Anita said and reached down to open her purse.

"Sold out, miss. Sorry."

Anita looked up sharply. The vendor was an older with a graying fringe of hair around his bald dome. Du her ingrained respect for her elders, she decided she wou treat him courteously. "Look, buddy," she snarled, "th whole county of Larson has less than five thousand people. The other school's base population is just as small. This pile of old rock seats plenty more than that! So you see," she concluded with just a touch of irritation and a gentle, only slightly condescending smile, "there's no way it can be sold out."

"Miss." The old man was jaded as well as sublimely sure of his facts. "Every available seat's been taken. I'm sorry."

"Sorry?" Anita's question was loud enough to cause people nearby to turn and look. Her hand snaked under the security bars and grabbed the front of the man's shirt. "Sorry?" she repeated with rising heat. "I'm afraid that's not good enough! My brother is playing in this game—which, thanks to your incompetence, has already started. The man I'm going to marry—if I can talk him into it—is coaching this game.

"You're going to look around very carefully back there and find a ticket you previously overlooked and you are going to sell it to me. Understand?"

She let go of the ticket seller's shirt and he smoothed it down as he stepped back out of reach. "Okay, lady, okay. I'll find you a ticket." As he fumbled through the stacks of material on his counter, he seemed to regain enough courage to ask peevishly, "Who the heck *is* your brother, anyway?"

"Jesse Valdez. Remember the name."

The man stopped scrabbling around and looked at her with something she didn't recognize dawning on his face. "Your brother's Jesse Valdez? Does that make you Anita Valdez?"

When Anita nodded, the man reached into a cubbyhole at the end of his counter. "Well, why didn't you say so? Here's your ticket right here. No charge." He handed over asteboard strip. "Enjoy the game," he said and med down the cover of his window.

To her surprised delight, she was on the aisle in the fifth row, nearly at the middle of the field. "Sold out, ha!" she muttered as she sat down, her eyes already scanning the field.

"Well, hey—Anita! You came! He said you— I mean, how are you?" It was Bill Wiatrek, the Larson High principal; Anita answered his greeting absently, her attention riveted elsewhere.

The stadium seats were filled with boisterous fans of all shapes and sizes. Down on the field, the sidelines were crowded with uniformed players, officials, media people and anyone else who could manufacture a reason to be granted a pass to be there. They all could have been petrified tree stumps as far as Anita was concerned.

Her brother was on the edge of the playing area, ready to rejoin his team on the field. He was listening to Jack. As she watched Jack's slow, confident hand movements describing something to Jesse, Anita's heart spoke again. Loudly. It said without a molecule of doubt that she loved Jack Hayden. Loved him just the way he was, loved him enough to risk the danger that life held for everyone. Loved him enough to let go of her roots, to reach beyond them and give both Jack and herself a chance to grow and find happiness ahead by facing whatever came next, wherever it came.

Love was worth any risk. Love must be cherished and expressed while you had the chance. Love lived with your beloved, of course. She'd miss Larson, but where Jack was, that's where her heart was. That was home.

Anita gazed at the field in astonishment. The damned fools were continuing to play their stupid game! She was on fire to share the news of her decision with the man who mattered—and now she was stuck with nine thousand extra people with another agenda.

She crossed her arms and slumped in her seat. She
to wait through the whole dumb game—it would prob
go on for hours.

Anita sighed. She'd be lucky if she caught Jack getti
on the bus to go back to Larson an eternity from now.

She sat bolt upright, livid with impatience. She didn't want to wait an eternity; she'd already waited long enough. She wanted Jack and two gold rings, one for each of them. She wanted his babies in her arms and his crazy foot-in-mouth ramblings sounding in her ears and his earth-shattering kisses burning her lips. As far as she was concerned, *that* was the kind of stuff that ought to last an eternity, not dumb championship games.

"Pretty close so far," Bill Wiatrek said, a little loudly.

Anita stared at him. *What? Oh. Yeah. The game.* "It is?"

"Score's tied and the game's almost over," Bill explained. "Those Eagles are tough on defense—Jack can't figure out a way to break Jesse loose."

"Jack..." Anita sighed and returned her attention to the dear, wonderful hunk on the sidelines. Even from this distance, she could tell he looked a little thinner, there were a few new lines etched beside his mouth and his hair needed cutting. In other words, he was gorgeous. She realized vaguely that Bill Wiatrek was still talking nonstop.

"Excuse me, Bill," she cut in. "My mind was on... Well, what were you saying?"

The principal's mouth twitched. "I said, isn't it the darnedest thing you ever heard of, but that's the way he wanted it."

With the patience of several saints, Anita managed to control her annoyance. "That's the way *who* wanted *what,* Bill?"

"I thought you knew—the school board offered Jack a three-year contract extension." Now when he had something valuable to impart and should have babbled uncontrollably, Bill Wiatrek imitated the Sphinx.

a fixed him with an interrogatory glare the FBI
ı have admired, but a fist of fear squeezed her heart.
d he take it?" she finally demanded.

Bill barked a laugh. "That nut case? No. He said he was ,ıving up coaching to sell shoes. Said maybe he'd teach math for us."

The crowd roared; Anita and the principal politely rose to their feet with the rest, but Anita, at least, paid no attention to the action. "Teach math? That's crazy—he's a wonderful coach. He shouldn't quit."

Bill's nod was accompanied by the sort of smile usually worn by proud parents when their children do something especially clever. "I agree, but we couldn't persuade him to change his mind. He said he was staying put, whether we wanted him to coach or not. Said he had to prove it beyond words, whatever that means."

Anita mulled it over. Added it to her companion's smile. Factored in the ticket seller's about-face. Ignoring the crowd still standing around them, she sat down, leaned back in her chair, crossed her arms and fixed the principal with a steady stare. "He said that, huh? Anything else I should know about?" she asked at last.

"I always said you were the smartest girl in Larson," Bill said with another pleased grin, then nodded. "He put a down payment on a house. The Kosub place behind the school. Nice—three bedrooms. Oh, and he traded in that fancy red car of his."

"His car? What for?"

"Four-wheel sport/utility vehicle."

Anita speared Bill with her eyes. "Why?"

"Well, he asked me and Vern what we thought you'd like. I've always thought you ought to drive something better suited for those rural emergencies you answer."

Later, Bill Wiatrek would struggle for words to describe Anita's appearance. Radiant didn't go far enough. Transformed, maybe. Transcendentally beautiful, for sure. "Illuminated by the awesome power of love" would have said it best, but high-school principals have to watch thei utation for poetic flare.

Anita was already standing in the aisle, one foot in m air, when Bill tried to stop her descent with a hand on he arm. "The game isn't over yet, Anita."

She shook away the nuisance detail and the hand, her full attention on the man on the field. "I have to go to him. I have to apologize. Explain. I have to promise him... *everything*. I have...to..." Her voice faded as she descended the steps.

"You can't go out on the field yet, Anita—he's busy!" Bill yelled at her back. "He has to win us a state championship first," he finished in a normal voice. No need to shout when you're talking to yourself. He stood up and pulled a yellow hat from his pocket. He waved it several times in great arcing motions.

Vern, who was standing on the sidelines holding a 35-mm camera, saw the yellow dot in the sea of Badger blue and lowered the prop to his side with relief. He returned Bill's wave, then hurried over to whisper in the ear of the man wearing his lucky navy blazer.

Jack started to whirl around, but the photographer halted the coach's turn with difficulty. "Didn't you tell me to make you stick to your game plan?" Vern asked.

"Yes," Jack muttered, "but dammit, I've been waiting my whole life for her."

"And we've been waiting twenty years for a state championship. Proceed as planned," Vern ordered. "You've only got two and a half minutes left."

Jack looked at the field and signaled a time-out. When the team came over and surrounded him, he whipped out his pen and applied it to the paper on his clipboard. "Watch and listen carefully, guys, because it's a little complicated..."

The inspired defense won Larson possession of the ball within thirty-five yards of the other team's goal line. Danny led the Badgers twenty yards downfield like Sherman

...ing through Georgia, then called a trick play that ...gled the defense's formation and allowed Jesse to slip ... the end zone and leap high in the air to catch the win-...ng touchdown pass.

The cheering crowd grew silent when he didn't get up after the play. They watched in apprehension as a small dark-haired woman ran onto the field and pushed between the players to get to the fallen hero.

Anita knelt beside her brother, running her hands and her eyes expertly over his body, automatically checking for injuries, even as her heart pounded erratically—not in fear for her brother, she noted. From being so close to Jack.

"Jesse, can you hear me?" Anita's anxious question produced a shaky nod.

"Yeah. Breath knocked out. Okay."

Anita turned to look into Jack's face—his wonderful, adorable, haggard, worried face—for the first time in too darned long. "Oh, Jack—" She breathed out his name in a sigh that had the referee scratching his head and clearing his throat.

"Er, could we get back to the injured player?" the official suggested.

Anita inspected Jesse once more, then sat back on her heels and smiled at her brother. "Well, Jesse. Are you going to let a little thump stop you or are you going to finish the game?"

Jesse jumped to his feet, waving to accept the cheers of the crowd. He and the other boys lined up for the last play, while one official guided the love-struck couple off the field. He deposited them safely out of bounds, then ran back to finish his work.

"Anita," Jack managed to say while his eyes hungrily devoured the sight of her beloved face. "Are you sure Jesse's okay?"

"He's fine."

"Are you . . . okay?"

"I am now." Especially since his arms were holding her tight, their bodies touching.

Fabulous tingles were running through her from point of contact. Those sweet, teasing, tantalizing ting She was gazing into wonderful, warm, green-gold eyes. have a lot of things to tell you, starting with—I love you.

Far in the distance, there was a mighty roar like an ocean. Jack only heard the words Anita whispered before he said, "I love you, too, Anita. You do know that, don't you?"

Anita nodded. "Yes, Jack."

"I'm quitting coaching, Anita. I want to stay in Larson. I always did. I thought you'd want me to make more money, for kids and stuff, but I want to love you here." His eyes were great green pools of desire and promise.

"I heard about the house and the car."

"I had to show you how I feel about you and Larson. My mouth can't be trusted to say things right."

"Are you sure, Jack? About Larson? I'll be glad to go to Indiana or anywhere else with you. My family, my roots... They'll go with me."

"Anita, I love you. And I love Larson. I've always wanted to be part of something..." He struggled, one finger stroking the side of her face. "Something steadfast and normal." His lips lifted in a quick smile. "There'll be plenty of room for Jesse to stay with us."

She was swinging that silky black hair from side to side. "Jesse's going to Indiana. I went to see the campus and signed the papers. You were right. I can't deny him or Danny such a great opportunity.

"And Jack, about coaching—"

"What?"

"Don't give it up. You have a special talent for it and kids like Jesse need the things you provide—guidance and discipline and self-confidence."

"You mean it? Hey—I'll sell shoes. Anything to have you love me, Anita."

"I do. Stick to coaching."

Jack picked her up and swung her around, then set her on her feet as his knee buckled. He pulled her against his nice, mostly strong, slightly flawed body and spoke from awless heart. "I love you, Anita. I want to be with you rest of my normal life." He looked at her with those rm, wonderful eyes. "Anita, that house... It's big nough for a couple of kids."

A little crease formed between her eyebrows. "That's something we've never talked about, Jack. You won't mind having mixed kids?"

He looked blank. "Mixed? I kind of wanted one or two of each sex, but if you want to mix them up, I guess—"

"Jack, you idiot! What am I going to do with you?" Her smile broke through her pretend exasperation.

He grinned and the tingles reached earthquake strength. "I suggest you take me on a very long honeymoon. Where shall we go?"

"Would you shut up and kiss her, Coach, so we can commence celebrating our victory?" a voice asked impatiently.

A chorus of agreement made the couple tear their attention from each other long enough to look around. A semicircle surrounded them: Larson players, the opponents and their coach, a man in a suit holding a big trophy, a TV crew and most of the town and county of Larson, Texas.

Anita applied pressure with the palm of her hand against his cheek. "Yeah, Coach," she said softly. "Shut up and kiss me."

* * * * *

It's our 1000th Silhouette Romance™, and we're celebrating!

And to say "THANK YOU" to our wonderful readers, we would like to send you a

FREE AUSTRIAN CRYSTAL BRACELET

This special bracelet truly captures the spirit of CELEBRATION 1000! and is a stunning complement to any outfit! And it can be yours FREE just for enjoying SILHOUETTE ROMANCE™.

FREE GIFT OFFER

To receive your free gift, complete the certificate according to directions. Be certain to enclose the required number of proofs-of-purchase. Requests must be received no later than August 31, 1994. Please allow 6 to 8 weeks for receipt of order. Offer good while quantities of gifts last. Offer good in U.S. and Canada only.

And that's not all! Readers can also enter our...

CELEBRATION 1000! SWEEPSTAKES

In honor of our 1000th SILHOUETTE ROMANCE™, we'd like to award $1000 to a lucky reader!

As an added value every time you send in a completed offer certificate with the correct amount of proofs-of-purchase, your name will automatically be entered in our CELEBRATION 1000! Sweepstakes. The sweepstakes features a grand prize of $1000. PLUS, 1000 runner-up prizes of a FREE SILHOUETTE ROMANCE™, autographed by one of CELEBRATION 1000!'s special featured authors will be awarded. These volumes are sure to be cherished for years to come, a true commemorative keepsake.

DON'T MISS YOUR OPPORTUNITY TO WIN! ENTER NOW!

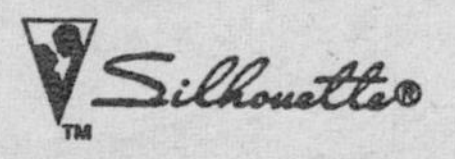

CELOFFER